A Thunder of Guns

For Jeb Sullivan, racked with despair over the deaths of his wife and child, there seems little to live for. He seeks to join his lost love in the afterlife, challenging any thug, hoodlum and quick-draw to achieve that end.

But his arrival in Driftwood changes everything and soon he's in love with the feisty, man-dressing TJ Griffin and accepts the sheriff's badge. Now his daily battle is to stay alive. In this lawless corner of the West, a tinderbox of tensions flashes into war. It's a storm of anger that Jeb must quell: it's a thunder of guns. . . .

A Thunder of Guns

Clay Starmer

A Black Horse Western

ROBERT HALE · LONDON

© Clay Starmer 2013
First published in Great Britain 2013

ISBN 978-0-7198-0662-9

Robert Hale Limited
Clerkenwell House
Clerkenwell Green
London EC1R 0HT

www.halebooks.com

The right of Clay Starmer to be identified as
author of this work has been asserted by him
in accordance with the Copyright, Designs and
Patents Act 1988

Typeset by
Derek Doyle & Associates, Shaw Heath
Printed and bound in Great Britain by
CPI Antony Rowe, Chippenham and Eastbourne

CHAPTER ONE

For Jeb Sullivan – his 160lbs clad in dust-soiled denim, his dark, hurt-filled eyes shaded by a Stetson – life now revolved around new routines. His horse was ridden miles by day, his passage ever westward. When light seeped out of the sky, he'd make camp.

Right then, with dusk dressing the land with shadow, he mused on a nearby copse. Soon, inside that sprawl of cottonwood, he let the mustang drink and then tethered its leathers to a low-slung bough. With the saddle off, he knelt at the water's edge to ponder a notion that had plagued him for days. He scooped water in cupped hands, sating his aching thirst. Splashing at his stubble-coated face then, he gave a nod.

'Now's the time,' he uttered softly, 'to be together again!'

Then he set to a meal. He garnered jerk beef, lit a fire for coffee and with his meal concluded, he sat with his back against a tree base, smoking and cursing the world.

Morning, noon and night – all could get to hell. Nothing mattered; nothing owned a beauty or a joy. Life – God's gift, Jeb used to believe – was an unbearable purgatory. Let it end!

*

In time, exiting the trees, Jeb sank to his knees, drew his Colt .45 and set the muzzle end to his temple. Right now, in dusk's leaking light, he considered it all with an intensity of one whose grief brought him to the point of madness.

The loss of your only child could do that – an aching hurt that few knew or could appreciate. Jeb swallowed down sobs and fought guilt and despair that rose from his guts as bile.

A momentary distraction and Jonny had gone. A normal day; Jeb on a break as deputy marshal of St Joseph Law Department back at the neat home he shared with his beloved wife and child. Why he'd removed his gun-belt and hung it on the back of a chair couldn't really be explained. But that mattered little in the end. Jonny, with his parents engaged in a lingering embrace, struck with the inquisitive speed of a six-year-old. With his father's revolver to hand, the rest was tragic history,

Afterwards, as Jeb cradled his dying child and smothered the boy with kisses, he could little imagine how his life would change. With Jonny buried, a solid marriage crumbled with startling speed. Jenny blamed Jeb, of course. Her way of coping was to turn her utter grief into anger and lash out at the man whose firearm had blasted the life out of their child. Jenny's rage and despair then turned inward. She existed in a tormented world of intense silences; her days spent wandering alone along the banks of the St Joseph's River. Several people saw her that morning, weeks after Jonny had been laid to rest – all testified that she'd jumped from the Washington Street Bridge. With his wife and child gone, Jeb sold his home, handed back his badge and with a saddle-bag of dollars, he just rode away.

Now, a year on, at this spot on the plains and with his finger squeezing at the trigger, Jeb mused on the other feeling that had gripped him that day. He'd felt followed and watched. Often he'd back-trailed, scanning intently. Finally, he'd dismissed it as paranoia and ridden on regardless.

Jesus, Jeb implored, *shoot and get it done with.*

But it didn't happen. He willed it to – a sight more pressure with his finger and a slug would slam into his brain. Jeb cried out with frustration and sought to garner the guts to go ahead with his suicide. Finally, hanging his head and dropping his gun, he sobbed steadily.

His weeping halted quickly, though. A sound drummed out of the distance – that familiar iron-hoof clatter of a fast-driven horse upon the parched, dry land. When the beast showed, a sweated-up bay with a black-clad man in her saddle, Jeb stared down the barrel of a levelled Winchester rifle.

'Listen, son of a bitch,' the man growled through chipped teeth. 'I won't shoot; I just want money!'

Jeb's dark eyes narrowed. He noted Chipped-teeth's shabby attire and fear-pinched pallor; he eyed the tremor in the man's hands that made the rifle buck in his grip.

'I'd set to be alone,' Jeb offered with a shrug. 'I've gotten tough stuff to dwell on.'

'Jesus H Christ.' Chipped-teeth's eyes flashed angry. 'Ain't we all?' His face muscles twitched and he snarled, 'What ails you hasn't a fly's hide on my troubles.' He spat at the grass before snapping, 'Money, cur. Bring it slow and easy!'

Jeb's apparent calm belied an inner rage. 'My wife and child died,' he said softly. 'I'd reckoned to—'

'Shut goddamn up!' Chipped-teeth's face tensed now with stress. 'I ain't got time for this.' He jabbed the rifle. 'I'm for dollars, not listening on a bitch dead wife and scum cur kid!'

Jeb's sigh, air passing through barely parted lips, had presaged the end of men. In nine years as a US marshal, he'd stood toe-to-toe with many and none of those had survived.

He took his time, though, choosing a ruse. He lifted his Colt, slid it to its holster then got to his feet. He half-turned then, jabbing a hand at the copse. 'It's in the trees, in my saddle-bag. It's close to six thousand dollars, I'd reckon.'

Chipped-teeth's grin presaged a whoop. He slid to ground, growling, 'Walk steady . . . I'll go with you.'

Jeb, a smile playing at his own lips, locked Chipped-teeth with death's own stare as he uttered, 'Come get it, bastard!'

Even as he said it, Jeb hauled up the Colt with slick-fast speed. With his left hand flat-palming the hammer, he drilled a slug out through smoke, flame and noise. Soon, with the last birds wheeling out of the trees and the gun's bellow fading to quiet, Chipped-teeth grunted and dropped to his knees. He spilled the rifle, his hands now clawing pathetically at the bloody mess at his guts. Lastly, he slammed face-down on the grass, twitching once before assuming that rigid pose that only the dead achieve.

Time and Jeb's efforts took care of the rest. He got the

corpse up and lashed it across the bay's saddle. He readied his own mount then, eventually looping the bay's reins about the sorrel's saddlehorn. With that done, he slapped the body on the back before shoving a hand into his own saddle-bag.

'Six thousand,' he grunted, pulling out a wad of dollars, 'I wasn't lying.'

With the greenbacks shoved back, he hauled out a map. With this opened, by the light of a struck match he picked out a nearby town called Driftwood.

'We go there,' he said to the cadaver as he hauled himself onto the sorrel. 'Maybe it's bounty on your head, son of a bitch!'

He pulsed with hope now. He saw a future – albeit a short-lived once. Sure, he couldn't blast himself but others would happily do it. He'd take on the scum of the West: robbers, saddlebums, drunks and thugs. He'd slay some along the way but the law of averages said he'd face a man too many and would perish himself. That didn't matter. He'd be with Jonny and Jenny.

Let the dogs go for me, he incanted as he crossed the now night-clothed miles, *I'll blast them all to hell.*

CHAPTER TWO

Driftwood's night lamps led Jeb in. Now, his horse halted where Main Street met the plains, he studied a town seemingly in the grip of lawlessness. Horses bunched at the rails, the boardwalks creaked under the weight of men and to a backdrop of bellowed curses and piano tunes, a pair slugged it out in the road's dust whilst another dispatched slugs at the star-dotted sky.

Jeb tensed and sighed, inching a hand to his gun butt, but his caution wasn't needed. The fistfight quelled, and a moment after, bedding his gun, the shooter staggered into the shadows.

To ground now with a grunt, Jeb mused on Driftwood's incongruity. It just didn't add up; the numbers of folk swamping this town should have ensured a constant flow of dollars. Yet the settlement looked to be in decline – wall paint peeling in the wind whilst buildings enough stood behind boards and chains.

Yet some places traded – clearly chief amongst these, a three-floored hostelry called the Regency Palace Saloon. That drinking den's batwings clattered loud and often, whilst a hum of noise drifted out to the road. Elsewhere on

10

Main Street, light flooded out through a livery's flung-open doors and a steady stream of custom moved in and out of a property bearing a sign: Williams' Bathhouse & Barber's Shop. Jeb's guts churned with relief; nothing right then seemed more inviting than a soak in a tub to ease out the aches of the trail.

First, though, he'd the corpse to deal with. He lost no time unleashing the body and heaving it over a shoulder. He scanned for a jail, noted a singed wood sign across the street from the saloon and headed there. He ascended the boardwalk steps with a grunt, pushed past a group of watching men, then, setting a boot to the jail's closed door, he watched as it crashed open. As the door settled against an inside wall, Jeb tipped the body off and sighed as the corpse slammed onto the boards with a resounding bang.

'God alive!' The man who leapt out of the chair behind the law office desk, eyes wide behind horn-rimmed glasses, stared aghast at the corpse before he gasped, 'What've you goddamn done?'

'I blasted that son of a bitch!' Jeb shrugged, taking in the man's grey hair and age-creased skin. 'You're not the sheriff?'

The man's groan spoke of a body pained. A hand pressed to his guts soon proved it. 'I've ulcers. You dropping dead men don't do them any good.' He sighed, muttering edgily, 'I'm the mayor of this dung hole. The name's Tom Collins.'

'I'm Sullivan.' He proffered a hand. 'Jeb Sullivan.' After the mayor shook, Jeb said with a nod, 'And that cur I killed?'

'Joe Corrigan.' Collins' eyes widened. 'Why'd you kill him?'

'He tried to rob me – that was his first mistake.'

'His first mistake . . . there were others?'

'He bad-mouthed my dead wife and child. That settled his fate.' Jeb sighed. 'He chose to level a gun at a man riding through. We all make our choices and pay for them.'

Collins sighed. 'Yeah, Frosty Hayes is making a choice now.' He jabbed a hand at the door and Jeb turned as a man staggered in.

The entrant, tall and muscle-bound, his sun-darkened features taut with rage, glared from corpse to Jeb.

'You've blasted Joe!' he roared, those words scented by liquor. 'Corrigan owed me twenty bucks. That debt's to be paid so you'd best show me some greenbacks!' He lurched forward, took a fistful of Jeb's coat and spat, 'Pay, bastard!'

Jeb's driven knee, slamming into the drunk's groin, brought a quick result. The man fell, hands clutching at his hurt. On the floor, he groaned and rolled. He sought relief but didn't get it. Jeb followed up. He booted the man's back, bringing more cries. Dragging the wounded bruiser to his feet now, Jeb forced the winded, hurting sop out through the jailhouse door, off the boardwalk and into the road. When the beaten one crashed into the dirt, Jeb glared at a semi-circle of men nearby.

'He gets in my face again, I'll really hurt him!'

Back in the jail with the door slammed shut, Jeb said testily, 'That's Joe Corrigan, eh? It seems he was a man with enemies?'

'When you do poker with rough sorts,' said Collins with a nod, 'you'd best pay up if you lose. Corrigan didn't.' He sat again and added drily, 'Why, Sullivan, did you bring him here?'

'On the hunch he'd be known; I wondered on bounty too.'

Collins sighed. 'I told you, he was a drunk and a gambler. The only people who wanted him were those he owed money to.'

Jeb noted the jail's bare wood walls. 'You're kind of lacking in posters. You've no bounty going about these parts?'

'Who knows?' Collins's grin lacked mirth. 'Our last sheriff used wanted posters to light the stove.' He sat and sighed. 'Sheriff Lyndon ran out six months ago. I can't get a replacement since!' He eyed the corpse. 'It'll cost the citizens to bury that sorry body!'

Jeb produced a twenty-cent coin. He flicked it onto the desktop and grunted, 'Your gravedigger's pay – I wouldn't want to cost the taxpayer!' He turned to leave but Collins's call halted him.

'Hey, Sullivan, are you stopping in town?'

'I'm not sure. A couple days of easy living certainly appeal.' He shrugged before saying, tiredness layering his words, 'I've ridden a distance and this is the first town for a time.'

Collins's eyes sparked behind those rims. 'You stay about here, it might not be easy living for you. Debts don't die with the man about these parts, as you've seen. You slay a feller and he owes another then you're beholden. That twenty Hayes sought is nothing against what he owes other men.'

'That's no issue for me,' Jeb said curtly. 'Corrigan's debt is between his dead flesh and them he sat cards with.' He tipped a finger to his hat brim. 'Good day, Mayor Collins.'

When he'd gone, Collins dragged a whiskey bottle out

13

of a desk drawer, uncorked it with his teeth and took a swig. When the liquor burned at his guts, he gasped before settling his thoughts firmly back on Sullivan. 'So long,' he muttered, 'You've done your bit for Driftwood, now ride on out!'

In the Regency Palace Saloon, Aaron Auger battled to tell his tale. He fought against the raucous waves of noise – a mix of shouts and the pounded piano keys. Finally, when a brief hiatus came and the saloon quieted suddenly, Auger set boot to foot rail, sloped against the counter and sought to gild the story. He nodded at the Palace's owner, Ralph Hartford, before saying, 'He's some hot-shot gun-fighter from out East!'

Hartford, fifty and weary, groaned. After three years at the saloon, he dwelled on Driftwood's troubles and his own vexed wedlock.

Driftwood's woes: lawlessness owing to a lack of a sheriff meant those locals that endured just prayed for better days. As for marriage to one Amy Du Pres, it'd been a huge mistake. She, a settler wife whose husband died to an arrow, fell for Ralph. Shortly after they'd wed, though, her demands grew. He'd sold his chicken farm when Amy sought the saloon. Now she asked for something he wasn't sure he could deliver. She wanted the saloon on the market and for them to set out East to purchase a teashop.

Ralph uttered a soft curse. This trouble in town just worsened. He'd employed a guard, but that man lasted just two days before fleeing. Right now, only the sawn-off behind the counter could quell trouble, supposing Ralph could even summon the courage to use it.

Damn Collins, Ralph silently inveighed, *you promised a new law in Driftwood. Well, I don't see a sign of it!*

Quelling his ire, Ralph anchored Auger with a withering glare. The young man, slow of thinking but with snooping skills aplenty, walked a fine line. Anyone who gossiped as the kid did was playing a risky game.

'Aaron,' Hartford growled. 'You've got big ears and a bigger mouth. You'd best keep both closed about this saloon.'

Auger grinned. 'Heck, my news must be worth something?'

Hartford drew a beer and set it on the counter. He liked the kid and his sickly pa. Old man Auger, his health bad since the death of his wife, couldn't control his son now. Ralph did what he could – occasionally the odd dollar or a gratis drink.

'Sup that, then get home,' Ralph said testily. 'I don't like you about this saloon when it gets late.'

Aaron nodded and carried his flagon to an empty table. There, he sipped whilst keeping a keen eye on comings and goings.

Hartford mused on the rows with Amy and her demand for Boston. He didn't want to go – loved Driftwood and its people – but there was no end to the town's troubles. He'd give it a month more, he avowed. If things didn't improve, he'd consider Amy's demands to re-locate. His heart sank. To exit Driftwood, where he'd been born and raised, would be the toughest decision of his life!

Sam Griffin, half a century a liveryman, possessed skin the hue of ochre and creased like wood bark.

'You're fresh off the trail?' the ageing horse-tender said as Jeb appeared at the barn doors. He waggled a gnarled finger, 'Still, a wash and shave and I reckon you'd scrub up.'

Jeb's lips inched to a grin. 'I already saw the bathhouse. I'd say that's my first stop after here!'

Griffin smiled back. 'He'll launder your gear if that's your want.' He winked. 'Cal will shave you too, with a cut-throat.'

Jeb turned to the sorrel and bay. Both now stood in the street with reins trailing. 'The stallion's mine. I'd look to lodge the beast for a couple of days.'

Griffin approached the horses with a confused look. He tapped at the bay's rump then. 'This is Corrigan's mare. What the hell—'

'He don't need it.' Jeb shrugged. 'He's dead in the jail. I reckoned to trade the horse for livery fees.'

Griffin frowned. 'Maybe his folk got a say about that?'

'He's got some?'

Griffin cackled. 'No, he was a solitary bum and that's goddamn lucky for you.' He led both horses in and then said, 'I'll trade the bay for your sorrel's fees. You owe me nothing.'

'That bay's worth more than feed and care for my horse,' pressed Jeb then. 'I'd say it amounted to a bed for me too.'

Sam jabbed a hand at the hayloft. 'What would you say to—'

'No,' snapped Jeb. 'I've lived weeks at the hide end of rough and I want some goddamn comfort.'

Sam nodded and, still gazing up at the hayloft, he growled, 'TJ, get down here now!'

When a youth showed, slim-bodied in duster and

wide-brim, Jeb gasped, exasperated. 'Well, old man, about the lodgings?'

Sam stayed silent whilst the youth, jabbing a hand at Jeb's chest, snarled, 'It's all want, ain't it, son of a bitch?'

Jeb's tensions peaked to rage. He'd lost wife and child; ridden five hundred miles and suffered every step of it. What with Corrigan and Hayes dealt with already, he wasn't about to accept a sassy insult from a two-bit kid. He threw out a hand, gripped the youth by the throat and squeezed tightly.

The boy turned colour, his pallor a hue of blue before he gasped, 'Oh, Jeez, please let me—'

'Stop that,' Sam Griffin bellowed. He eyed Jeb edgily. 'You don't beat on a gal, no matter if she cusses you out!'

Jeb gasped. He shook his head, eased his grip off the youth's throat and watched, bemused, as the youngster dropped to knees to hold there, spluttering and coughing. With the hat spilled, auburn locks flowed long.

'A woman,' Jeb exclaimed. 'I just didn't—'

She looked up, a slim, pretty-faced creature with damnation in her eyes. In her twenties, Jeb guessed. She mouthed a curse.

'I'm sorry, ma'am. With that garb I'd swore you a boy!' He sent out a hand to help her up but she brushed his overture away.

Standing, she moved close, a hint of a grin at her thin lips.

Jeb, offering a nod, had his head jerked back as she landed a punch to his jaw. He grunted and reeled away – unbalanced more by surprise than pain – but quickly got his composure. He stood straight and waited. When she punched again, a haymaker wheeling in, Jeb deftly stepped aside. Her fury committed her to failure. With her momentum thrown forward, her punch powering through air, she stumbled across the barn with a speed that quickened as Jeb's boot connected perfectly with her backside. A moment later, slamming headfirst into one of the barn walls, she slid to the floor and lay, facedown and cursing.

Jeb sought conciliation one more. He strode across, grabbed a handful of her duster and dragged her to her feet.

'Please,' he implored. 'I'm sorry, damn it. Why won't you—'

She clawed fingernails to his face and only desisted at her pa's stentorian call.

'TJ, enough! Get to the house and stay till I say other.' She stalked off and Sam sank to a hay bale. 'She's been like this since her ma died. A drifter did it eight months since. It was an accident, him drunk, but TJ's against any stranger since that day.'

Jeb nodded. 'I'm sorry. As for me, I'm no saddlebum.'

'I'm Griffin as the sign says; the fiery gal is TJ . . . short for Teresa Jane.' The liveryman looked troubled. 'Her being tough's good in a way. Mind, I don't want her killed too.'

Jeb slid off his hat and sighed. 'I'm Jeb Sullivan. I lost my own wife and child about a year back. The loss takes some getting used to, although you never do, of course.'

Sam stood, lifted a key off a nail in a post and passed it to Jeb. 'Here, there's a shack at the west end of Main. It belongs to me. You use it whilst you're in town.'

Jeb smiled. 'I really am grateful.' He replaced his hat and departed the barn then.

Sam, standing between the barn doors, watched him go. In time, he attended to the horses. He worked distracted, though. In fifty years of horse care, he'd seen all sorts. But this Jeb Sullivan left him perplexed.

'I sense something about you, Sullivan,' he said, moving both animals into stalls. 'I've just got to work out what it is!'

CHAPTER THREE

By the light of the jail's two lamps, Driftwood's gravedigger Hank Waverley perused Corrigan's body. He stood straight then, his look grim.

'It's said about town,' Waverley grunted, 'that Corrigan got blasted by some famous gunfighter.'

'Goddamn Auger,' Collins snapped at that. 'If I'd a sheriff I'd have the boy locked up for gossiping.' He gave a depressed sigh. 'A man named Jeb Sullivan shot Corrigan. He rode—'

'No,' cut in Waverley. 'It's said the gunfighter's took on the Griffin shack.' Waverley shrugged. 'Looks like this man Sullivan's staying a while.'

Collins's guts turned. Sure, Sullivan shot Corrigan and then punched Hayes into the street easily enough, but other men thereabouts needed a more cautious approach. Collins mused on Jake Fraser then. That man – a hawker for the Circle C – bore an aura of trouble but the last sheriff's timidity ensured no inquiry. Most likely, if Fraser was wanted some place, his poster burned in the stove like all the rest.

Auger's gossip, which the sheriff often followed with as

much interest as any, decried Corrigan's debt to Fraser to be six thousand dollars.

Yet, now he thought about it more, Collins felt content. He'd warned Sullivan of the risks inherent in staying in Driftwood. If the man chose to ignore the warning, it was his funeral!

'You've told him,' pressed Waverley unerringly. 'Hell, all the debts Corrigan racked up, too.'

'Yeah,' said Collins, grunting to his feet and looking exhausted. 'You'll take Corrigan to your place?'

Waverley nodded and left. When he rapidly returned, he had his son aside him and they lugged the body out through the door. Collins moved to close the jail then. He doused the lamps, grabbed the keys and stepped out to the boardwalk. With the jail door secured, he pocketed the keys and gazed sombrely at the increasingly liquor-fuelled antics of the men crowding Main Street. He looked intently then towards Driftwood's western edge. A beam of light sprayed out of the Griffin shack's front window and Collins resisted an urge to stride there and remonstrate with Sullivan again. Instead, descending the boardwalk steps, he battled through the crowd to reach his home. His mind raced all the way, though, a host of ideas sparking as he moved.

In a hut abutting the Circle C quadrangle, Jake Fraser inhaled on a cigarette and eyed his surviving gang member intently.

For his part, Billy Hall, twenty and doubt-filled, stood grim-faced, a shoulder pressed against one of the bunkhouse walls.

'It's best to stay here,' Billy growled. 'We've got it made

– wages, food, no law hassling us. Why'd we risk all that?'

Fraser, his eyes sparking, spat angrily, 'Stay here – doing lickspittle work each stinking night?' He stood, dropped the smoke butt and ground it under a boot. 'Six weeks and I'll have that money.' He jabbed a hand out. 'We're shackled to the end now, you and me! Hell, we stick close – us against the world!'

Billy stifled a groan. He cursed, his life soured. A year before, in North Bend, Montana, with his brother Reece, they'd done odd jobs to survive. Then Fraser showed. In no time, Reece, enraptured by Fraser's wild talk and wilder ways, had agreed to join a gang. Others were soon recruited – six in all, including Billy. Fraser moved into the crumbling hut Billy and Reece shared and from there, he planned.

Weeks after, choosing the Montana settlement of Clancy for the gang's first daylight bank raid, Fraser led them to hell. It was a disaster from first to last – the townsfolk well-drilled against potential heists. Whilst the gang exited Clancy's branch of the Mid-Western Union Bank with some fifteen thousand dollars, that was as good as it got. They saddled to a hail of bullets. Five of the gang perished, including Reece, before their horses moved. By a miracle, Billy and Fraser escaped Clancy unscathed. The money, fluttering in the breeze, curtained the street as they fled town.

They'd ridden flat-out for days, pursued by a posse. With that shaken off, they'd ridden weeks more until reaching Driftwood. Here, luck played a hand. Lomas sought workers and Fraser acquiesced. It was soon clear why: one roper said a cattle drive was due. Lomas, in Dodge and with a heck of sale dollars to hand, would be worth robbing.

'They're two dozen ranch men and Lomas as well,' Billy growled edgily now. 'There ain't a chance in hell we'll—'

'I've talked in some ears,' Fraser cut in with a smirk. 'Men waver. I'd say a few might be persuaded.' His grin slipped as he snarled, 'Wade Lever's riled more than me about this brand.'

Billy's face darkened. Lever, the middle-aged foreman of the Circle C, had an abrasive temper and he'd taken against Fraser from the start. Right now, relations between the two were like a tinderbox waiting to catch light at any moment.

'We're taking risks with that man,' Billy protested. 'Hell, we ride into Driftwood when we should be guarding the herds; then there's that Corrigan business. It won't be long afore someone's tongue's loose enough for Lever to find out.'

Fraser tapped a finger to the gun strapped at his right leg. 'If Lever keeps pressing I'll fix it some other way!'

Billy looked bereft. 'Ain't we got trouble enough?' He spoke with passions fired, his grief over Reece still raw. 'Clancy was crazy. To heist Lomas at Dodge is stupid. We'd die for sure!' He jabbed a hand at the window. 'Even if we pulled it off, where'd we hide that none would look?'

Fraser, rage in his eyes, none the less spoke now with an unaccustomed solemnity. 'Now, I'll tell you 'bout that. 'Cross the border is Tiahuanaco. There, a man can shake off any past. With dollars to hand we'll be kings in this El Dorado!'

Billy's disquiet rose as bile. It was just another of Fraser's crazy tales. The man existed in a world of fantasy – get-rich schemes and dreams like Tiahuanaco. Nothing bore reality. Yet people died, just like Reece, due to Fraser's delusional ideas.

'I want to go lawful,' Billy snapped. 'I want a little farm, marry and raise kids. I don't want—' His words ended abruptly as Fraser lurched across and slammed a fist to his gut. As Billy dropped, battling tears, Fraser brooked no dissension.

'You swore to the gang,' he hissed. He dragged Billy upright and spat into his face. 'Once in, never out – that's my motto.' He slammed Billy into the bunkhouse wall. 'You go against me, Billy boy, you'll get sorry, I've told you that enough times.'

'Please,' Billy gasped, 'I didn't mean—' A back-handed slap choked off his pleading.

'Now, enough talk. What I say, you do. Any more lip and by God I'll beat you stupid.' Fraser stalked to the door. 'Tonight,' he said testily, 'we set to Driftwood. I want my money.'

With Fraser gone, Billy sighed, depressed. He recalled Corrigan in an alleyway with Fraser's knife to his throat.

'Don't kill me,' Corrigan begged those few days before. 'How'd I find six thousand dollars?'

'Get robbing,' Fraser had spat back. 'You've little time and if I don't see my pay I'll cut you into strips.'

Billy ached for Reece now and the life they'd shared before Fraser appeared. Poor but happy then, they'd earned their way by honest toil. But that was gone – ahead now lay a fugitive life and likely sudden, violent death. Unless he escaped Fraser's insidious grip, Billy knew, he existed condemned. He weighed up the risks. Any plan to flee, with Fraser in pursuit and vowing bloody revenge, filled Billy with terror. To stay, though, meant certain demise.

'I will leave,' Billy hissed at the hut's still-open door. 'Someday soon, Fraser, you'll be out of my life for good!'

CHAPTER FOUR

With Driftwood's clocks inching past 9 p.m., Jeb studied his reflection in a mirror on the shack's rear wall. He nodded, content. Washed now and shaved, he showed half-presentable. The time he'd spent in the Bathhouse & Barber's Shop proved beneficial in different ways. He'd soaked in a hot tub, all his saddle ache eased. Whilst he'd bathed, Cal Williams brush cleaned Jeb's clothes then pressed the shirt of creases. Later, he'd cut Jeb's hair and worked skilfully with the cut-throat razor.

Jeb mused on the shack now. This three-roomed property came with provisions aplenty; his short stay in Driftwood would be a sufficiently comfortable one. Considering the unlit stove, then, Jeb decided to dine out.

Soon, ignoring the bellowed insults of drunken men, Jeb kept to the street's sides until he reached the intersection with Harper's Way. Midway along this road, he sighted Malone's Eat House. This place, its door ajar and its window filled by light, possessed a few cloth-topped tables flanked by chairs.

Malone, a portly, bearded Irishman, wore a welcoming grin.

'Come away in with you,' he greeted. 'There's time for custom, right enough. What'll it be, friend?'

Jeb sat, studied a menu and then ordered steak and potatoes followed by apple pie. Later, supping delicious coffee he listened as Malone reinforced the mayor's solemn entreaties.

'Watch your back,' Malone nodded, his smile slipping for the first time. He noted the skull inlaid on Jeb's gun butt then said laconically, 'But that might be advice you don't need telling.'

'Frosty Hayes,' Jeb said with a frown. 'I already had a set-to with that man. Any worries there?'

Malone dropped into a seat and, to Jeb's pleasure and surprise, he'd gotten a brandy bottle to hand.

'Something,' he said with a nod, 'to welcome you to town.'

With a sizeable addition of liquor in his brew, Jeb grinned. 'Thanks. I appreciate it.' He added pointedly then, 'Folk have been kind since I got to Driftwood: Sam Griffin for one.'

Malone's eyes widened. 'You've met his gal, TJ?'

Jeb nodded and put a hand to his jaw. 'She packs a punch.'

Malone chuckled but then his look was serious. 'It was bad about TJ's ma; gunned down by some drunken scum.'

Jeb let the brandy-laced coffee warm his guts. 'She's never gotten over it, I guess?'

'TJ just gets worse,' said Malone with a sigh. 'She keeps cussing strangers, she'll join her ma in the graveyard.'

Jeb, quaffing the last of the drink, reached a hand to his pocket and produced coins. He set them on the table, stood and then strode to the door.

'Where're you going, Sullivan?'

Jeb stopped, spun about and shrugged. 'Your brandy's set me in mind for a drink. I've a powerful trail thirst.'

Malone shook his head and pointed at a shelf bearing a host of bottles. 'My stuff's better than the Regency . . . and cheaper!'

This sealed it. An hour later, Jeb, Malone and his wife Mary seated at a table, the night passed in bonhomie and drink. At midnight, tiredness dragging his eyelids shut, Jeb chose to leave.

'You're fine people,' he said with a nod. 'I truly am obliged.'

'About Hayes,' said Malone edgily. 'Just watch the shadows. He's that kind of trouble.'

Soon, walking slowly along the night-blackened distance of Harper's Way, Driftwood's unnerving quiet suddenly struck Jeb. With those sounds of lawlessness quelled – no raucous shouts or gun blasts emanating from Main Street – only the low hum of wind and the rattling call of a loose, buffeted board kept the town from complete silence. Jeb sighed. As the night had progressed, Malone's door closed, the liquor flowing and their talk and laughter filling the room, they'd simply not noticed the drunken din besetting the settlement. Likewise, as the town emptied of people, they'd not appreciated that the town had quieted either.

Jeb mused on Driftwood's people now – that resident population including Sam Griffin and Malone and his wife. They restored Jeb's faith in everything. Frightened and struggling as they all were, they still proffered generosity. Jeb groaned now, crippling weariness hitting him. Yawning, he thought longingly about the untroubled night's slumber in a proper bed that he'd soon enjoy. He strode quicker now, getting onto Driftwood's central thoroughfare, but then he halted.

He scanned Main Street. To the road's eastern end, the livery and its surrounding buildings sat back in dark. In the other direction towards the shack, light still streamed out of the saloon. Moving that way, Jeb noted the man outside the swing doors who lent over the boardwalk rail smoking a cigar.

'Howdy,' Jeb proffered, drawing close. 'I'm Sullivan. I'm stopping in town a few days.'

The man nodded. 'I'm Ralph Hartford; this is my place.'

Jeb couldn't suppress another yawn. 'I'm dead beat. A full night's sleep won't be regretted and that's for sure!'

Hartford's look was penetrating. 'I'd reckon gunfighter miles are tough on a man.'

Jeb's look was vexed. 'A gunfighter, you say?'

'I hear you blasted Joe Corrigan,' grunted Ralph, 'I also. . . .' He trailed off but then added, 'A kid's in town that spins yarns. You did kill Corrigan, though?'

Jeb nodded. 'I had to, Mr Hartford. Corrigan tried to rob me at the end of a gun.'

Hartford did his best to smile. 'Driftwood's quieted early. It makes a change.' He stood straight and shrugged. 'Corrigan was a drifter who set into town and never left. He lodged where he could and without paying, mostly.' The saloon owner flicked his cigar to the street. 'I've got to shut the saloon. Stay safe.'

He stepped away, pushing through the batwings, and as they stilled and the saloon rapidly darkened, Jeb set to cross to the shack. He paused briefly, though, sensing that

Hartford was watching.

Hartford did just that. In the now unlit long bar, he peered over the top of the batwings, a gnawing worry in his guts. He couldn't put it into words – just the feeling that some evil, as yet undefined, lurked late in Driftwood's streets that night.

In the road, Jeb sighed and moved on. He bristled as he walked, aware of some kind of threat but certain that it didn't emanate from Ralph Hartford.

He recalled what Malone said earlier: danger lies in the shadows. He halted, inched about and stared into the dark at the street's edge. Suddenly, the wind's gusting persistence quelled. Into this brief hiatus fate intervened. He heard the slightest scuffling noise. He waited, tense now, hand settled on the butt of his Colt.

Flame parted dark and a hellish roar signalled a sent slug. Dropping fast as hell, Jeb pressed his face to the dirt, gasping as a slug ripped into the air above his pressed-down body. It missed, slamming into a wall on the other side of the street. Upright fast, his gun to hand, Jeb battled back. He saw two blurred forms charging out of the shadows. The voice that howled out he recognized instantly.

'Bastard,' Frosty Hayes bellowed. 'Beat on me, you'll die.'

He shot again, this bullet screaming across the distance to spit soil close by Jeb's foot. There'd be no other attempt. Jeb, his right arm levelled, slammed a finger to his trigger and dispatched a slug through an eruption of flame and smoke. When the bullet struck, it pummelled into Hayes's forehead.

Hayes's life ended in a spray of blood and brain. When his useless corpse fell, hitting Main Street's dust with a thud, Jeb set his sights to the other.

Down on one knee, Jeb's next gun blast sent lead to guts. He who died next, staggering with a scream as the bullet ripped through his stomach, tried desperately to stem the tide of blood. Finally, gurgling with pain and horror, he staggered away until he reached a rain barrel at the street's edge. There, he slumped, his head dropping into the barrel's fill of dust-topped water. How he perished – whether by bullet or drowning – mattered little. Die he did, though, his thrashing legs stilling, his body limp.

Upright now on that street reeking of gunsmoke and cordite, Jeb heard a dog howl down an alley and then watched aghast as Driftwood ignited into life.

Ralph Hartford appeared on Main Street first. With the batwings crashing, the saloon owner bustled down the boardwalk steps and approached Jeb at a jogtrot.

'I saw it all, goddamn it,' Ralph bellowed as he moved, 'I saw the sons of bitches jump you from the dark.'

Others now showed. Rapidly, with maybe sixty people bunched on the road, Jeb's disquiet peaked. When Collins strode into view, the mayor perused the two corpses before shaking his head.

'I'd have put money on Hayes wanting revenge,' he said. 'But I didn't think he'd seek to kill, or get Del Taylor to aid him!'

'A mistake,' Jeb said. 'They've learnt that the hard way.'

Collins shaped lips to answer but the arrival of Sam Griffin and TJ halted him. The ageing liveryman pushed though the crowd and jabbed a hand at the blood-soaked remains of Frosty Hayes.

'Goddamn,' he gasped. 'You blasted them both, Sullivan?'

31

Jeb didn't reply. He looked intently at TJ who, clad in a nightgown, stared piercingly his way. When their eyes met, however, she dragged her eyes to ground.

As Jeb mused on that, Hank Waverley and his son showed.

'Jeez,' the gravedigger blustered. 'What in God's daily name happened here?'

'I saw it all,' Ralph Hartford barked. 'Hayes and Taylor shot at Sullivan and both got what they deserved.'

Mayor Collins gave a resigned shrug. 'I'll take a report in the morning, Ralph. It'll be written up as justifiable slaying.'

Hank Waverly sighed. 'Keep this up, Sullivan,' he offered wryly, 'I'll be out of coffins.' He shrugged, adding, 'Hayes and Taylor were single. Drifters who'd no ties they spoke of.'

Jeb frowned. 'It seems single drifters attacking me's getting quite a habit about here!'

Waverley frowned. 'So is your killing of them.' He winked at his son. 'Chris, we'll get these dead to our place.' Soon, with the help of some of the locals, they lugged the bodies away.

In time, as people drifted back to their homes, Collins appraised Jeb with a look of resolve. 'You're in the clear, like I said; men what ambush out the dark ain't worth spit.'

Again, Jeb kept quiet. He pinned TJ with a penetrating stare but her returning look was harsh. When she once more dragged her gaze away, Jeb gave a groan. He departed then. Soon, inside the shack and with a lamp lit, he dropped despondently onto the bed.

As he lay, musing on so many things, Mayor Collins got busy.

'In the jail,' he said to Hartford and Sam Griffin. 'It's time for a meeting, I'd say.'

Later, TJ held in the street, staring at the shack, her eyes anchored on the door as if by dint of that she could see through to Sullivan. She couldn't, though, and turned to leave. Only near the livery did a sound break from her lips.

'Damn it, Aaron,' she spat angrily as Auger drifted out of the dark at the street's edge.

'He's a famous gunfighter,' Auger hissed. 'He's blasted three men today; hell knows who'll be next!'

'Maybe you; now get, you stinking skunk.' She bent, got a stone to hand and hurled it. It missed, clattering into a wall but it set Auger running. His bootfall pounded down the alley, finally fading as he neared his home.

TJ, clamping her stare to the shack again, proffered a curse.

'Famous gunfighter,' she sneered. 'He ain't that!' She spat at the road, knowing exactly what he was . . . or at least what he'd been. She went to the horse barn, to the chest lodged at the barn's rear wall. In this, earlier, she'd put the items she'd removed from Sullivan's saddle-bag – a heck of money – and the paperwork that revealed Sullivan had once been a US marshal!

CHAPTER FIVE

Miles to the west, sitting their mounts on one of the Circle C pastures, Fraser and Billy suffered. They'd endured the bitter vagaries of the last few hours – air getting steadily colder and then chilled more by the wind. To top it all, critters kept howling, skittering their horses. Finally, they'd eased their mounts behind a screen of mesquite to get relief from the gusts. Now they waited.

Fraser, cursing softly, gazed up to that fullest of spring moons. That orb, seemingly so close this night a man could just reach up and touch it, layered the mesquite with silver and heightened a host of trees in the distance. By its light, they'd see the approach of others.

'Say, Bill,' Fraser proffered, 'I've thought on what you said in the hut. I reckon you're right.'

Billy, shivering, gave a grunt. 'About the heist in Dodge being too risky?'

'Huh,' Fraser grunted, 'maybe. More on Corrigan and that son of a bitch Wade Lever. I think we'd best stay at our guard tonight – leastways till Lever gets his snooping done with.'

Billy's relief was audible. He sighed loudly, grinning in

34

the dark. 'Damn it, Jake, I'm sure happy about that. We could stay at the Circle C. We could work our—' His words stilled as the drum of hoofbeats carried across the cold land.

'Riders,' Fraser hissed. 'Goddamn Wade Lever!'

They reined up in a maelstrom of snorts, but their beasts' cries didn't drown Wade Lever's levity-layered words.

'I said so,' the Circle C's stand-in boss roared, slapping a hand at his leg. He laughed loud, adding, 'The curs have set to Driftwood. We ride and catch them. That'll be the finish of it!'

'Yeah,' growled a roper. 'The scum have had it coming!'

Fraser, cursing softly, rode out from behind the mesquite.

'You talking about me and Billy?' he said edgily. 'You calling us two scum?' He spat at the grass before jabbing a hand. 'Plead forgiveness, Lever . . . you and these other dogs!'

'Get to hell,' Lever snarled a reply, his eyes wide and hate-filled. 'I goddamn know what you're up to and I'll catch you at it. When that happens you're done with, you hear me . . . it ends!'

They all dragged reins, driving their mounts out of there with heels and shouts. When the noise of their departure quelled, only the wind's low moan and Fraser's spat curses were audible.

'Hear that?' he grunted after a time. 'He says we'll be done with.' He urged his horse on. When he yelled back, it chilled Billy's blood. 'When I'm done, Wade Lever'll be dead at my feet!'

*

Jeb, sliding between the sheets, got his head to the pillow and expected sleep to come quick. It didn't. In time, he sat up, rested his head against the wall and battled dark thoughts.

He felt depressed and on edge. His grief was still raw but Driftwood troubled him too. The town was a two-edged sword – the kindness of people like Sam Griffin and the Malone couple balanced against the underbelly of violence that resulted in his slaying of three men that day. He dwelled on TJ then and another emotion spiked. She plagued like an irritant itch. Mind, for all her feisty ways, beneath her abrasive exterior she obviously suffered terribly over the death of her mother.

'She hates me,' he whispered now, that thought wounding, though it shouldn't have mattered. He liked her; she hated him. That was clear. A shame, he mused. She was a handsome woman. He cursed again. He'd resisted any other woman since the day his wife died. On the trail, it wasn't a problem, of course. In Driftwood, with TJ close, however, it was a different thing.

You swore to suffer, he inveighed now, *forever alone, never to know love or joy again till you die.*

Stumbling out of the bed, he knelt in supplication. He tried to pray but gave up as his body racked to sobs. In time, slumped and weeping, he willed help.

Show me, he intoned to Jenny and Jonny, exhaustion swamping him. He stumbled back into bed. *Tell me what to do!*

He slept then; felt nothing – neither joy nor pain!

In the jail, Mayor Collins, Sam Griffin and Hartford drank in silence. Collins finally broke the quiet.

'If Sullivan keeps this up,' he drawled, 'all the goddamn troublemakers will be dead!'

'I didn't see a like of it,' Hartford opined. 'How Sullivan shoots leaves no doubt. He blasts true; keeps nerve under fire.' Ralph shrugged. 'Auger's right . . . Sullivan's a gunfighter!'

'It's not that,' Sam Griffin retorted testily. 'I seen the skulls inlaid on his Colt. I've seen the way he fought with my gal. He's something but he's no hired gun!'

'What, then?' Collins snapped. 'He's a bounty hunter?'

'Hell, no,' Sam growled, setting his mug aside. 'Sullivan's a skilled killer, right enough. I've had this hunch since I met him.' He got to his feet. 'If you ask me, I'd say Sullivan is, or at least I reckon he was, a—'

'Lawman,' barked the mayor and Hartford in unison.

'Yeah,' grunted Sam. 'He said his wife and son died. That would break a man whatever job he did.' He strode to the jail door then stopped. 'He's shot three thugs today. That slaying rate could change Driftwood's fortunes.'

'Talk to him, Sam,' Collins said pleadingly. 'After all, he's living in your shack!'

'If I'd lost my wife and child,' said Sam pointedly, 'it'd take more than a liveryman's pleads to make me stay in Driftwood.'

'Ask him,' Collins pressed as Sam left, 'to take a badge.'

'I'll try,' said Sam as he stepped onto the silent Main Street and turned to walk away. 'As God is my witness I'll try!'

Seth Lomas, waiting in the Circle C quadrangle, bristled as Wade Lever and the trio of ranch-hands rode in. Soon, all of them off-saddled and Seth beckoned Lever into the ranch house. In the parlour, Seth dispensed whiskey and passed over a shot glass.

'Well,' the cattle owner drawled. 'What happened?'

'They were out by the herd.' Lever's eyes sparked with anger. 'I'll catch them, boss, I swear it.'

Lomas sighed, his emotions mixed. He didn't want to lose any more men but to have workers abusing his trust was tantamount to spitting in his face. Any ranch boss inflicted brutal and summary justice to men who drew wages but failed to do their duties.

'Where'd you hear they were failing me?' Lomas growled now.

'A kid named Auger,' Lever said testily. 'I paid that boy a couple of dollars and he said that Fraser and Hall regularly ride into Driftwood past midnight and drink in the saloon.'

'Goddamn it, Wade,' the ranch boss snapped, 'I won't have ill feeling on account of what a half-wit who gossips for money says.' He quelled his ire and said more gently, 'Give up this idea that they aren't up to their work. They're good boys and they've served me well so far.'

Later, alone in the yard, Wade Lever nodded with certainty. He'd bring Fraser and Hall down. Maybe the townsfolk of Driftwood wouldn't disclose, mindful of retaliation, but Auger's tongue was loose. Auger spoke true, Lever was certain of that.

'I'll finish those bastards,' he growled as he set to the small shack he used, 'if it takes me from now till next goddamn year.' He spat at the dark earth. 'I'll do for those two scum curs, no matter what it takes!'

CHAPTER SIX

It was only an hour since dawn but already the air of the plains shimmered with heat. That day's sun, a hellish yellow burn, made a mockery of the bitterly cold hours they'd endured through the night before. Right now, sweating as they rode, both Fraser and Billy ached for food and sleep. They crew they passed on the way – ropers and punchers full of comments and sass – Fraser ignored. Later, with breakfast taken and both of them asleep, across the miles to their east, Driftwood bustled into life.

In the Regency Palace Saloon, Ralph Hartford swept vigorously as he mused. He'd slept little over the previous hours, unsettled by so many things ... not least his wife's barracking words.

'More dead?' she'd screamed when he'd returned from the jail in the early hours. 'We're out this hell town and you're buying a tearoom in Boston.' She'd spat bile then. 'You're a stinking hick fool and why'd I marry you I can't fathom.'

Ralph cursed and dwelled on Sullivan. Hell, if Sam could persuade that man to wear the law badge in Driftwood, all might change. He set the broom aside, got to the batwings and peered out at the very moment the shack door opened and Sullivan showed.

'Well?' Amy's bellow made Ralph turn. She stood on the stairs, adding with bile, 'You useless piece of hick Driftwood trash. Are we going to Boston or not?'

Ralph didn't answer. He just watched blank-faced as Amy stormed back upstairs. As she slammed doors to vent her rage, on Harper's Way Jeb settled into a chair at Malone's for breakfast. As he dined, content, things passed less cordially at the livery.

'He's a stinking killer,' TJ barked, shoving her plate aside in the small kitchen. 'Three men dead and you don't give a damn!'

'Corrigan, Hayes and Taylor,' Sam snarled. 'All thugs who set upon Sullivan, seeking to kill that man. What the hell choice did he have?' Sam nodded with certainty. 'With Sullivan about Driftwood we could end this town's troubles!'

TJ slammed a fist to the tabletop, sending plates and mugs jumping. 'You'd no goddamn right to rent the shack to that man; you'd no goddamn right—'

'You cuss again,' said Sam with fire in his eyes. 'I ain't chastised you for years but I wouldn't hesitate to do it again.'

With eyes sparking fury, she hissed through gritted teeth, 'He's a scum murderer. He's just like the bastard that—'

'No,' Sam roared lurching to his feet. 'He might be a heck of things but I wouldn't reckon him the type of filth that shot your ma.' He trembled enraged. 'I'm embarrassed how you've acted, Teresa Jane. I've let it go on account of you suffering over Ma, but it's got to change!'

She moved to go but he stilled her with a slammed fist.

'Sit,' he bellowed with steel to the word. She slumped back down as Sam yelled, 'How are you to set to marry and get me grandkids when you cuss out and try and fistfight any man you meet? God alive, gal, you've got to alter!'

She shaped her lips to protest but the fury in her pa's face kept her silent.

'The way you've treated Sullivan,' Sam berated, 'it's shameful.' He quelled his rage, said more calmly, 'His wife and child died, TJ. The man's living with that hurt!'

Her eyes widened and there was a definite quiver in her jaw. 'Wife and child,' she muttered softly. 'I didn't—'

'You never do,' cut in Sam. 'You're too busy blaming anyone for Ma's death you can't get close enough to see who they are.'

Tears pricked her eyes and her head dropped.

'I spoke with the mayor and Hartford last night,' Sam said bluntly. 'We all reckon there's something about Sullivan. He's sort of special, you might say. We can't let such a man through our grip without at least asking him to be sheriff!'

'Sheriff,' she gasped.

'Why sure,' said Sam plaintively. 'He's a—'

She stood, reached into her duster and dragged out a sheet of folded paper. She placed it on the table. 'He's an ex-marshal out of Missouri.'

Sam looked appalled. 'You stole it,' he gasped. 'In my living years I'd not stoop to that! I taught you better, gal.'

She raged now, dragging out of her coat a sackcloth bag into which she'd lodged Jeb's money. She slammed it on the table with a curt, 'Six thousand goddamn dollars he's carrying.'

A taut silence endured – a tension-layered hiatus through which TJ shook with anger and Sam stared transfixed at the paper and the bag. When he lifted the paper and unfolded it, he read a glowing reference from Jeb's boss at the US Marshal's Service. He threw the table aside then, grabbed TJ by the arm and hauled her into the livery barn.

'We're setting to the shack,' he roared. 'You'll get on your knees afore Sullivan, admit what you did and beg his forgiveness!'

She struggled like a wildcat but couldn't break her pa's hold.

'I'll not apologize to a scum killer like him,' she spat venomously. 'And you can get to goddamn hell, you . . . bastard!'

Sam followed through on his word. He dragged TJ into the livery barn where he lashed her hands to the rusting wagon wheel he kept propped against the rear wall. She struggled and wailed but that was as nothing to her howls when he reached for the length of birch stick. That whistled into pain, the bite to the flesh of her buttocks and legs producing gut-wrenching screams. So loud were her wails and pleads that people on Main Street stopped to listen, both appalled at the spectacle but also pleased. . . . TJ's truculent ways, admonished universally, had finally been addressed by her pa. Pressed at the livery barn's front wall, Aaron Auger snickered into his hand.

'Whip the bitch,' he kept saying, grinning inanely as he hopped from foot to foot. 'Call me a skunk, would she?'

With the punishment finished, Sam left TJ tethered whilst he calmed himself in the kitchen.

'Why do you hate men so?' Sam howled at one point, pressing his head against the kitchen wall and trying to stifle a sob of frustration and self-loathing. 'Why?'

'Hate,' TJ said in a hoarse whisper, sagging at her binds. It was easier that way. Hate meant you didn't have to love. How could she love any man when one of them had butchered her beloved mother? Better to despise and curse them to hell. She whispered then through parched dry lips, 'I don't love you, Jeb Sullivan.'

Her head slumped then; she knew the opposite was true.

Seth Lomas, crossing the deserted quadrangle, sought a discussion with Meredith. Lomas didn't make it to the chuck house, though. Halting, he watched intrigued as a man drove a horse down the stone-flecked road leading to the gallows gate.

Getting a hand to his gun, Lomas waited, tensed, but he soon relaxed. As the rider eased his mount into the yard, his first words put the ranch boss at ease.

'I'm a Wells Fargo courier,' the rider said hoarsely. 'I've ridden from Dodge with a letter for Seth Lomas, boss of the Circle C.'

'I'm he,' Lomas grunted. 'What the hell d'you—' He stopped short as the man proffered an envelope. Lomas took it, removing the letter inside and reading quickly. His lips twitched then, the edges curling to a grin.

'A gratuity and an answer,' the rider said curtly.

Lomas took a coin from a pocket and passed it over.

'The answer's yes,' he said with a nod. 'I'll be at Dodge in two days' time.'

The Wells Fargo man shrugged. 'Eight hundred – you'll deliver?'

'You reading my mail?' snapped Lomas testily. 'Get out of here afore I get angry.' As the Wells Fargo man left, Lomas nodded. He'd deliver the steers to the Dodge City railheads as requested. He'd make a decent profit, too. He re-read the letter, noting the details of his customer: Leonard Green of the Eastern Seaboard Meat Company. Lomas knew Green, of course, but Eastern Seaboard had regular suppliers. Perhaps one of those brands had gone out of business. Whatever the reason, Lomas would fulfil the order in the hope more beef requests would follow in the future.

'Two days,' he said with a nod. 'I'll do it, by God.'

Seething right now with self-hate, Sam un-bound TJ and sobbed for what seemed an age. Finally, his tears dried and his protestations of regret, too, TJ moved into the kitchen and picked up the letter and the bag.

'I'm sorry about how I've acted, Pa,' she said. 'Blaming the world for Ma dying ain't the answer.' She pondered on Sullivan's hurt. Hell, the man had lost a child as well as his wife. The pain couldn't even be imagined.

'Where you going?' blustered Sam, wiping a sleeve to his eyes.

TJ sighed. 'To say sorry to Sullivan like you wanted.' She went to exit the barn but halted as her pa called out.

'Ask Sullivan to dinner,' sighed Sam, 'tell him 8 p.m. I need to speak and I want him in a good mood when I do.'

TJ moved fast to the barn doors but then she stopped. Gazing out, she watched someone dash into an alleyway. She swore softly, knew instantly who it was. When Auger ran, hurtling into the alley, she cursed the halfwit for his

44

snooping and meddling ways. Quickly, though, she focused firmly on Jeb Sullivan. Her guts turned with nervousness now . . . or was it something else?

She swore again, her legs almost giving way. She went then, striding down Main Street and getting to the boardwalk steps close by the shack. Climbing these, she battled a sense of trepidation that urged her to turn and run. But she didn't. She got to the shack door and rapped firmly. She repeated this a few times and then, when no answer came, she turned to leave.

She gasped. He stood in the street, his look making her feel like she'd melt on the spot.

'What,' he growled, 'do you want, TJ?'

She gulped, flushed red and then blustered as she realized his eyes were boring into the sackcloth bag and envelope she held. 'It's not what it seems, Mr Sullivan . . . if I can just explain!'

He climbed the steps, slid key to lock and got the door open. He jabbed a hand then and said edgily, 'We'll talk inside, missy!'

Jeb dropped onto a seat; TJ held by the door, tight-lipped, her face pinched and pale. 'It looks,' Jeb said then, 'like someone's been through my stuff. Sit, gal, we'll talk.'

She shook her head. 'I can't, not yet. Pa beat me with a cane for going through your gear.' She moved forward and put the paper and bag on the table. 'I haven't touched a dime, Mr Sullivan. I'm most things people say but I'm no thief.'

Jeb proffered a look she couldn't define. He sighed then. 'You're read that reference, I suppose?'

'I read it.' She nodded. 'I wanted to say . . . about your wife and child that—'

'TJ,' he said more abruptly that he'd intended, 'I used to reckon it harder to make enemies than to make friends. A day in Driftwood has sure changed my mind. Hell, three men try to kill me; then I get on your wrong side. I never meant to—'

'It's my fault,' she barked, her face reddening again. 'My language is bad. That's mostly why Pa beat me.' She sighed. 'I know I did wrong.' Her face crumpled and she said, at the edge of tears, 'It's just, I get this nightmare of Ma dying. Sometimes I reckon she's alive and talking to me and I can't—' The words subsided to a sob whilst her head slumped.

Jeb shuddered. How could he tell her, or anyone else, of the visions that blighted his own nights? Times he'd staggered out of bed, drenched in sweat, his dreams filled with Jonny's seemingly living face and words. The boy raged, his message clear.

'No, Papa,' the boy always bellowed from the afterlife, 'don't you dare die!'

Jeb always howled his reply: how he missed his son.

'Stay, Papa – one day. Not now!'

'And Ma,' Jeb repeatedly sobbed.

Jenny – well, she never showed now. Last night, as Jonny's presence drifted out, there was just a sense of intense peace. It was as if, Jeb felt, she'd forgiven; a sense that however he chose to survive the years ahead, she'd given assent.

'I'll leave,' TJ said now, breaking Jeb's introspection. 'I hope you'll forgive me.'

He moved quickly, halted her by the door with a gentle hold of her wrist. 'Please, TJ, I'm sorry too.'

She blinked, confused, her eyes fixing onto his. 'You're

sorry . . . I don't—'

It happened then. Like magnets drawn, they clamped into a lingering kiss. Afterwards, Jeb stepped back and shook his head.

'Under that duster and wide brim, you're goddamn beautiful.'

She smirked. 'That's bad language. I ought to get a birch cane.' She winced with pain before saying with a spark in her eyes, 'Come to the livery at eight o'clock tonight. We want you for dinner.'

She fled then and Jeb swore. His heart pounded in his chest whilst a flood of longing coursed through his veins.

An hour later, close by the saloon and within sight of Driftwood's branch of the Kansas State Bank, a man on the cross-seat of a wagon applied the vehicle's break and licked his lips. He gazed now at the building abutting the bank – the boarded-up Assay Office. It wasn't a problem. Each month, a man from Grantville rode into town to assess the gold finds and apportion a price.

James Scott, grinning, shoved a hand under the cross-seat and dragged out a canvas bag that bulged with stones. Aged sixty, grey of beard, he'd enjoyed the fruits of risk. He'd worked abandoned and dangerous shafts in the Sabre Hills and found his fortune.

He set his attention to the saloon's batwings. He'd drink first, to wash down the dust, then set to the bank later to get the nuggets under lock and key. Shoving the bag of finds inside his shirt, he got off the wagon and strode up the boardwalk steps.

Soon, inside the sparsely populated Regency Palace, he sidled up to the counter and proffered a nod.

'A shot of whiskey, 'keep!'

Ralph Hartford bristled. He jabbed a hand at the slate behind the bar showing credit he proffered to the hard-up miners. Popular as Scott was, he didn't come running to pay his bills.

'You've got debt,' Ralph growled.

Scott, his battered hat removed, shoved a hand to the pocket of his soiled jeans. A moment later, placing a gold nugget on the bar he said with a wink, 'That'll cover the slate; plus pay for some redeye right about now, I'd say.'

Hartford, eyes widening and lips parted, grabbed for the nugget and shoved it under the counter. Standing straight then, he leant across the counter and hissed, 'Are you goddamn crazy? Never advertise what you've found!'

Scott shrugged and glanced about. Few enough folk populated the saloon right then, and all those that did seemed engrossed in their own affairs: a few were playing cards whilst others sat about the bar's tables, chatting and drinking. Only one person stared their way, the wide-eyed and attentive Aaron Auger.

Scott, dismissing the fool youth and his prying, growled, 'Well, is my debt paid and my drink on the way?'

Ralph reached for a bottle and glass. With a measure poured, he slid it across the counter.

Whilst Scott sloped to a seat with his drink, Ralph mused on the gold now in his possession. A sizeable enough nugget – it would likely pay Scott's debt twice over – it'd need cashing at the bank.

So the long-beard hit the rich stuff, Ralph mulled. *I guess wielding a pickaxe in them hills pays after all!*

*

With a handful of men still watching the herds, the rest of the Circle C crew gathered in the quadrangle. They'd been summoned back and now listened as Seth Lomas spoke. Fraser and Hall were there also – both roused from their slumber by the noise.

'Eight hundred steers,' Lomas informed them. 'The beeves need to be in Dodge by the eighteenth.' He jabbed a hand then and began to select the men for the drive. With that done – some twenty of the crew picked to go – Lomas nodded at Wade Lever.

'You'll manage stuff at the brand whilst I'm with the drive.'

Lever couldn't suppress a smirk. 'That's for sure, boss.' He threw Fraser a scathing glare. 'I'll manage stuff about here!'

'Fraser and Hall,' grunted Lomas then. 'You'll stay at the Circle C as well.'

Fraser's eyes flashed his anger. His jaw muscles twitched and he bellowed, 'Stay at the Circle C? What in hell d'you—'

'Silence!' roared Lomas. He jabbed a hand, fury setting across his features. 'No man questions my orders on this brand.'

Fraser, swallowing his simmering wrath, anchored the still-grinning Lever with a scathing glare but muttered sourly, 'Right you are, boss; we'll stay at the brand.'

Lomas said loudly then, almost to over-emphasize it, 'I've detailed six men to ride my wife and child to relations in Grantville. They leave within the hour.'

Before long, the drive crew readying themselves in bunkhouse and stables, just Fraser, Billy and Lever stood in the yard.

Fraser seethed. Denied of the cattle drive profit, shackled as he was to the brand, he'd have to content himself with what they could purloin out of Driftwood.

Lever, sensing his disquiet, baited with a growl, 'I've whispered in Lomas's ear. He's got the measure of you two.'

Fraser's own look was withering. He crossed the distance, snarling, 'Lever, keep pushing and you'll not like what comes back!'

Lever jabbed a hand angrily. 'I'll have you, Fraser. I know what you're at!' He strode away then, headed towards the cookhouse.

'The dream's over,' said Billy, trying to disguise the relief in those words. 'Forget Mexico!'

Fraser's eyes fired. 'No,' he snarled, shaking his head. 'Sure, we've lost the Dodge money but there'll be other chances. We start with the six thousand Corrigan owes!'

'To start with?' Billy gasped. 'You mean you intend to—'

'Nothing's safe,' snapped back Fraser, his eyes almost demonic now, 'until I've got the money I need!'

He strode off, leaving Billy leaning over the corral's top rail.

What am I still doing here? He silently inveighed. *Fraser's out for his own gain and you won't get a red cent. Hell, he'll kill you before you sight the Mexico border!*

Yet, despite guessing the blood fate awaiting him at Fraser's hand, Billy faltered still. He feared Fraser's vengeance if he fled. That man would come after him, and Billy recalled with horror Fraser's graphically described torture of those who'd betrayed him. Gulping now, Billy weighed up the respective perils.

Ride out of here, Billy rallied himself then. *God alive, if you don't you know you'll not live to regret it!*

CHAPTER SEVEN

With a fifth whiskey downed, James Scott battled to define the time by the saloon's tallboy clock. He now gave up, the redwood timepiece with its intricate hands refusing to stay still. When the room lurched too, he clutched his head in his hands and gazed blurredly at Aaron Auger.

'Say, boy,' he growled, 'what time does it say?'

Auger chimed back, 'Half-past three, Mr Scott.' Auger stood and leaned close. 'You need to be somewhere by now?'

Scott chuckled as his eyesight settled some and then he slapped a hand to the table. 'Dang, that's a fact.' He winked, then said softly, 'Yon bank don't close till five, isn't it?'

Auger nodded. 'It'll be quiet about now if you want to take money out.' The boy shrugged. His own business in the bank, usually the dollar or two here and there people proffered for gossip, he deposited in a savings account.

'Take money out,' slurred Scott with a snort. 'Hell, I ain't got two bits to rub together!'

Aaron frowned, confused. 'If you've no money to take out or none to put in, why'd the hell you want the bank?'

Scott patted a hand to his coat front. 'Gold . . . that's it.'

Auger's eyes sparked. 'You had a find, Mr Scott?'

Scott jabbed out with a finger. 'Some said me crazy going down them busted-up shafts. It paid me to do it, though!'

'And you got nuggets,' Auger enthused. 'You showed them?'

Scott nodded and winked. 'You bet it, kid!'

Aaron saw a chance. 'I'll help you to the bank for a dollar.'

Scott scoffed away the offer. He got unsteadily to his feet, felt the room sway then crashed to the boards. Rolling onto his back, he cursed then tried to stand. He couldn't manage it. At length, groaning, he gave up.

'OK, boy,' he grumbled, 'put me up straight and I'll take your help to the goddamn bank.'

Auger grinned, dragged Scott to his feet and, slipping a shoulder under the miner's arm, he aided him towards the batwings.

At the counter, Hartford felt a stab of disquiet. He'd proffered more whiskey than was healthy to the miner. Mind, he mused then, it wasn't his task to limit a man's liquor – least of all to Scott, who'd cleared his debt by means of a nugget with which Ralph would then make a sizeable profit. Ralph mused on Auger now, supposing the kid was up to some scheme. The last thing a drunk like Scott needed was Auger's attention. Ralph shaped lips to intervene, but a sudden clamour for drinks distracted him.

He busied himself with drawing beers and when he'd finished he glanced round. Scott and Auger were gone. He dispelled his worry, though. After all, no man, drink-beaten or not, would make the mistake of telling Auger their financial affairs.

Jeb, taking a break from exploring Driftwood's streets and alleyways, pushed through the door of Malone's Eat House. Inside, the Irishman proffered a welcoming smile.

'Hallo, Mr Sullivan. It'll be food you're wanting?'

Jeb dropped onto a chair. 'Just coffee – I'm invited to the livery to eat this evening.'

Malone's eyes widened. 'Dinner, is it?' he winked. 'Did Sam himself invite you or was it TJ?'

Jeb slid off his hat. 'She's different when you get to know her.' He sighed. 'If you can get past her shield.'

Malone poured coffee into a mug and brought it over.

'We heard about the shooting last night,' he said edgily as he set the mug on the table. 'Hell, we're pleased you're OK.'

'They jumped me out of an alley on Main Street,' said Jeb, sipping the strong, hot drink. 'They left me no choice.'

'The same as it was with Corrigan, eh?' Malone shrugged. 'Jeez, you're a single-handed killing machine!'

'Auger told you that too, I take it?'

'He tells everyone everything,' Malone shrugged. 'People need news even if isn't true.' He looked at Jeb coyly. 'You'd make a useful sheriff. I'm surprised Collins hasn't asked you already.'

Jeb held his tongue; he'd already considered that vacancy during his exploration of the town. That kiss he'd shared with TJ had lingered way beyond the physical act. After she'd left him at the shack, he'd tingled with a vigour that left him almost breathless. One kiss and he'd been smitten. He'd seek anything to keep him in Driftwood right now – and what better way than taking on the job of law in Driftwood?

'I mean,' Malone droned on, 'once those thugs get to hear you've blasted three men they'll think twice about coming here!'

Jeb, standing then, drained the last of the coffee, set the mug aside and strode to the eatery door. He halted before exiting, sliding on his hat before fixing Malone with a wary look.

'Some men might think twice,' he grunted as he opened the eat-house door. 'But others might relish the challenge.'

Malone shrugged. 'Auger says you're the fastest draw there is. Auger says. . . .' He trailed off because Sullivan was gone, the door slamming firmly behind him.

In the Circle C yard, Seth Lomas waited for all the drive crew to mount. When each was in the saddle, the brand boss mused on his wife and child. They'd set out on a buggy, guarded by six loyal and trusted men, to make the forty-mile passage to Grantville.

Lomas nodded, certain now. Sure, he'd validated Fraser and Hall against Wade Lever's condemnations the day before but he didn't trust those two night hawkers.

'Boss,' Lever bellowed out from across the yard, 'it looks like everything's set for the off!'

The ranch boss gestured, walked his horse to a quiet part of the yard and waited for Lever to get there. 'You've full authority in my absence, Wade. I trust you.'

'Fraser and Hall,' said Lever edgily. 'I know you don't—'

Lomas nodded. 'If they're abusing trust they'll suffer

for it . . . when I get back from Dodge. If there's proof, stay your hand till I return.'

Lever, grim-faced and with eyes narrowed, hissed through gritted teeth, 'Sure, boss, I hear you.'

Lomas smiled. 'Hell, I know I can always trust you, Wade.'

Lever walked away then, muttering softly as he moved, 'I'll wait for one thing: Fraser to lie in hell!'

It took time, owing to James Scott's sodden condition, but eventually, they completed the deposit. In line with bank procedures, the teller called the manager. He, the straight-faced Albert Lloyd, weighed the gold in his office and presented the chart for the cost per ounce. The figures were easy to discern – the bank bought gold at two dollars an ounce less the assay rate. They sold what they bought from the miners and made a tidy profit.

Later, a wad of bank notes to hand, Scott pushed Auger away.

'Get gone, kid.' He shoved a one-dollar note over and watched as Auger exited the bank.

Albert Lloyd shook his head. 'You OK, Mr Scott? You know we had killings in town – maybe you should set back to the hills?'

The long-beard belched, shoved the bills into a pocket then staggered to the door. 'Goddamn whiskey,' he grunted as he shoved his way outside. 'I've earned it!'

Lloyd stared fascinated at the pile of nuggets cluttering his desk. For this fortune, James Scott was three thousand dollars richer. Lloyd mused now on the previous day's killings – three men blasted by this drifter called Jeb Sullivan. He shook his head. Word about town was that if

Sullivan remained in Driftwood, one could only wonder at what carnage he might be involved in next.

Lloyd cursed softly. The lawlessness that had beset Driftwood had now escalated to gunfights and deaths. Sullivan's actions in slaying three thugs might end the rowdiness but it could also spark an orgy of trouble. As for Scott . . . well, anyone in Driftwood right then needed wits. To be drunk and in possession of dollars was neither sensible nor safe. Given that the gossiping Auger had helped Scott in collecting his gains, it seemed more vital than ever that Scott didn't linger in the town.

Lloyd stuffed the nuggets into a bag, which he shoved into a safe. He sighed then, both satisfied and relieved. Let James Scott risk the small fortune he'd accrued. Albert Lloyd wouldn't make that fool mistake!

CHAPTER EIGHT

Jeb caught up with Auger after a couple of hours. The kid slipped like an eel, seemingly everywhere and nowhere at the same time. On questioning locals, Jeb got to Auger's last sighted position to find the boy had moved on. When he did trap Aaron, it was by the town's picket-fenced grave-yard, the young man holding a bunch of picked wildflowers to hand.

'For my ma,' Aaron said softly. 'I miss her a lot.'

Jeb's rage dissipated fast. He'd resolved to confront the gossiping boy, to scare the young man to death if need be. Right now, though, he felt only pity. He watched as Auger stepped through the gate, knelt and arranged the flowers before a headstone. When Auger bent to kiss the grass over the plot, Jeb's guts turned. He felt Auger's loss almost as acutely as his own.

In time, Auger stepped onto the road and said, 'You wanted to see me, Mr Sullivan?'

Jeb sighed. 'Listen, boy, I just heard you'd been putting it about town I'm some hotshot gunfighter.' He spoke without heat, his words edged with care. 'I know it's prof-itable to say tales folk want to hear but I'm no gunfighter

. . . I'm just a plain man!'

Auger nodded. 'You can shoot, though! Hell, you've killed three men already.'

Jeb, battling a new spike of disquiet, decided on a different approach. Maybe, with the likes of Auger, the best way was to follow the crowd. He reached into a pocket and produced a two-dollar coin. He held this out towards Auger, who grabbed it.

'What d'you want to know?' He didn't let Jeb answer. Grinning, he added quickly, 'TJ's done cooked for you. She was singing right enough. I listened out back the livery!'

Jeb sighed. 'Is that it?'

Auger nodded and stepped away. Then he halted, glancing back, eyes glinting in the sprayed-down light of a lamp. 'A Wells Fargo man stopped by town today. He says Seth Lomas at the Circle C is headed to Dodge City with eight hundred beeves.'

Jeb shrugged, the significance of the information lost to him.

'Wade Lever didn't go on that ride,' said Auger. He stepped back towards Jeb and said softly, 'He's the Circle C foreman and he's a powerful hatred for Fraser and Hall.' He shrugged. 'When Fraser hears you blasted Joe Corrigan he'll get a hatred for you!'

'And I suppose,' grunted Jeb, 'you'll do the telling?'

Auger wore a pained look. 'They'll hear from another if it ain't me.' He nodded once more. 'Corrigan owed Fraser six thousand dollars. When Fraser finds you killed Joe he'll call for you.'

Jeb nodded, aghast that the amount of his money in his own possession matched exactly with Corrigan's card debt.

'Thanks,' he grunted to Auger then, 'for the warning.'

With Auger sprinting off, his pounding footfalls soon quieted, Jeb set to leave himself. He paused briefly, though, as Auger's words drifted back out of the shadows.

'It's the saloon just past midnight,' the young man yelled. 'That's when Fraser and Hall show!'

In time, having washed in the shack before his dinner at the livery, Jeb stood on the boardwalk and watched as Auger gravitated through another Driftwood evening crowd. A font of the settlement's happenings Aaron Auger might be, Jeb mused, but the kid walked a risky line. Then his thoughts turned to Jake Fraser.

'So I owe you money, eh?' he grunted as he stepped down onto the dust of Main Street. 'Well, come and goddamn ask for it!'

They sat their stilled mounts at the Circle C's eastern border. Here, where the Sabre Pasture gave out to the vast, flatland plain, the air reeked of cattle and dust as the herd moved in a bellowing procession into the night-blackened distance. When the last lowing quieted, close to two hours later, Fraser proffered a grunted curse.

'Damn it!' He slapped at his arms, trying to drive out the biting cold. 'We could set after Lomas – stay hidden till Dodge.' He spat now, dismissing his own suggestion. Lomas, a seasoned rancher, would post a guard to ensure they weren't followed. 'The cattle money's lost,' he admitted edgily. 'We'll ride to Driftwood at midnight and I'll get what Corrigan owes!'

Billy stifled a groan. Fraser hadn't changed. He was still hell-bent upon profit at any cost – most likely, that'd be himself and Billy in a grave.

Billy tried to steel himself to make a bid for escape. He mulled over staying awake after one of their night shifts, sneaking out of the bunkhouse whilst Fraser slept on and putting many miles between them. But always those horrific tales about Fraser's bloody retribution caused him to falter. He pondered sombrely on Wade Lever then.

'You reckon they'll snoop on us again tonight?' Billy asked sourly. 'He seems determined to catch us out!'

'He can get to hell,' Fraser snapped. A match flared as he set it to a built smoke, the flaring flame seeming to emphasize the harshness of his eyes. 'We've lost a fortune,' he growled, 'I won't lose another. We'll wait a while then set into Driftwood.'

Fraser dragged reins then, galloping his mount in the direction of the remaining herd.

As he rode, Billy grimaced. It didn't seem to matter now whether or not he left or stayed; he'd die either way. Yet, Billy reasoned as he got his own horse moving, at least by riding out on Fraser, he'd attain some semblance of honour. He'd end his days trying to flee evil; if he remained at Fraser's side he'd only be giving the man's wickedness credence.

Jeb waited nervously outside the livery doors just before 8 p.m. but Sam Griffin's cheery call put him immediately at ease.

'Come along in, Sullivan. I've a spot of brandy set by.'

Soon, in the livery kitchen, Jeb sat and accepted a drink. He sniffed the aroma of cooked food and considered Sam over the rim of the brandy glass as the liveryman dropped to a chair.

'It's good of you, Mr Griffin, to share your meal after

the trouble I've caused about town!'

'Trouble, you say?' Sam's eyes sparked. 'Blasting hood-lums isn't trouble; that's public-spirited and to the benefit of this town!' He looked uneasy now. 'I'd say trouble was a livery gal going through a man's saddle-bag.'

Jeb shrugged. 'TJ apologized.' He tensed, wondering briefly if Sam knew about the kiss. He decided, though, that TJ wouldn't have mentioned it to her pa. He added, 'TJ and I came to an understanding.'

Sam frowned. 'Those dollars you've got, they need to be in the bank.' He shrugged. 'Else I've a safe in my office.'

Jeb dragged the bag out of his shirt. 'In your safe; I'd be happy with that.' He passed the money over and watched as Sam scuttled off. When he returned, he re-took his seat and rubbed his hands together vigorously.

'OK,' he said, his eyes widening, 'I've summat to ask and I don't rightly know how to put it. . . .'

Jeb shrugged. 'Straight out is usually the best way.'

Sam did. He asked; then he pleaded. Afterwards, he drawled, 'The sheriff's wage isn't brilliant but there's a house attached. Well, what d'you say?'

Jeb sighed. 'Yesterday,' he said sombrely, 'before Corrigan set to rob me, I set my gun's muzzle to my head and aimed to blow out my brains. Then I killed Corrigan and it all changed.'

Sam looked confused, 'But how—'

'I couldn't do it,' Jeb said. 'I couldn't kill myself so I set to Driftwood hoping some thug would do it for me.'

'Three men tried; you don't seem in a hurry to die.'

'Everything's changed,' said Jeb. 'I'll die, for sure, but not any time soon.' He drained his brandy and said with a nod, 'I've met too many decent people in Driftwood and I'd like to repay their kindness. I'll take your sheriff's badge.'

Sam beamed. 'Goddamn it, that's good news. Wait till the mayor hears.'

'Wait till the mayor hears what?' TJ, sashaying into the room, had replaced her usual masculine garb with a flowing, flower-patterned dress. Whilst Jeb gawped, Sam's jaw dropped.

'Dang, gal,' he spluttered. 'I can't recall the last time I seen you as pretty as that!'

TJ tugged a hand nonchalantly to the dress's hem. 'This old thing,' she said edgily. 'I just minded to see if it fitted is all. Well,' she said pressingly then, 'what's the mayor to hear?'

'Sullivan's our new sheriff.'

TJ's reaction to the news – the slightest gasp – she quickly subsumed with an outward calm. She lightened the hours that followed then. Chatty, ever smiling, only her eyes betrayed any negative emotion. A few times, they sparked with a definite fury.

They locked gaze once, Jeb aching then to have the time and space to talk. He gulped and battled his own aroused emotions. He yearned for her with each passing minute but there wasn't a thing in hell he could do about it!

CHAPTER NINE

It was just past 11 p.m. when they lashed their horses to a rail outside the Regency Palace Saloon. Billy looked along the street's length, surprised at the lack of people in Driftwood this night. Where usually men thronged street and boardwalk until the early hours, right then only a few wandered towards their horses.

'Something's not right,' Fraser growled, 'I ain't seen the town like this since we set here.'

'I'll tell you why,' a voice piped from the boardwalk shadows. When Auger stepped into view, Fraser moved with speed. He leapt up the steps, grabbed a fistful of Auger's coat and dragged the young man into an alley.

'Jeez,' Fraser growled, slamming a fist to Auger's guts. With Auger howling, Fraser raged, 'Why'd you speak to me, halfwit?'

Blinking tears and bent double, Aaron gasped, 'I saw you ride in. I've news . . . it's important, too.'

Fraser dragged the young man upright. He glared at Billy then, who'd held by the horses.

'Get here, Billy boy!'

Hall, moving with hesitant steps, now got close.

'This dung-brain says he's got stuff I want to hear,' barked Fraser. He applied a swingeing slap to Auger's face and growled, 'Speak, halfwit . . . what you got to say?'

Aaron faltered. He'd been sure of himself; moreover, he'd felt certain Fraser would pay for the news about Corrigan's death. At this moment, though, with the Circle C hawker proffering violence, Auger's convictions dissipated fast. He gulped and shook his head.

'I'm sorry, Mr Fraser. I never meant to bother you.' His eyes watered and he tried to ease away. Fraser hit him again and Auger sobbed. 'Corrigan's dead. He got blasted by a quick-draw what's set into town.'

Fraser, with a stunned hiss, loosed his hold. As Aaron scrambled away, scuttling further along the alley, Fraser raised a hand to tip back his wide-brim.

'Corrigan's dead,' he said edgily. 'That best not be true.'

Auger's voice called from the shadows now. 'He that shot Joe – Jeb Sullivan – he's lodged at Griffin's shack.' Auger walked edgily out of the dark, a hand outstretched, the palm turned upward. 'He killed Frosty Hayes and Del Taylor too. Hell, he's blasting folk all over town and he doesn't break a sweat.' Fear still churned Aaron's guts but his want of dollars steeled him through. 'My news is worth something, ain't it?'

To Billy's amazement, Fraser dragged a coin from a pocket. With this pressed to Auger's hand, the halfwit ran.

'Sullivan,' Fraser growled now, 'owes me six thousand.' He turned, jabbed a hand in the direction of the shack and snapped, 'I'll go see him. I'll show what happens when you blast a feller what owes greenbacks to another!'

Billy, his body racked by a shudder, mused despondently on Auger's revelation. Not the fact that Corrigan was dead; that didn't surprise him at all. No, it was the presence of a quick-draw in Driftwood – a man sounding proficient with a gun and whom Fraser, crazily, sought to confront.

'Goddamn it,' Billy barked, indignation overriding all of his trepidations, 'this man Sullivan's slew men enough already. He might be anything: gunfighter, bounty hunter.' Billy's eyes flashed determined as he growled, 'We don't need that kind of trouble!'

Fraser battled an urge to lash out. He ached to confront the man in the Griffin shack; he also seethed with a need to beat Billy Hall within an inch of his life for more impertinent questions. He did neither, though. Stilling his ire, he decided to bide his time. What Hall said possessed some sense. Hell, the drifter had the blood of three men on his hands and Fraser sure wouldn't be the fourth. He'd make enquiries; he'd find out what he could about this drifter before deciding how to get his money.

'OK, Bill,' he drawled with a nod. 'We'll tread wary till we know who the bastard is and what he wants.'

Fraser cursed at plans shattered like shot glass. In the space of a day he'd lost the sixty thousand dollar cattle drive money and the six thousand Corrigan owed him now hung by a thread.

'If this feller's fast at the draw,' Billy dangerously pressed on, 'I'd reckon it best to forget that six thousand. Hell, you try and get it you'll—'

'Goddamn it,' barked Fraser, grabbing a fistful of Billy's shirt and applying a backhanded slap that drew blood. 'You don't turn yellow on me, Billy Hall!'

'No,' Billy gasped, tasting blood. 'I'm aside you!'

Fraser loosed his hold, saying edgily, 'We'll stay and get

what we can out of this dung-pile town. Tonight we drink; before Lomas gets back from Dodge City we strike!' He moved out of the alley and onto Main Street with Billy meekly following. Later, inside the virtually deserted Regency Palace Saloon, they got beers to hand and settled into chairs on the raised section.

They drank in silence awhile, only the low hum of voices or the occasional ballad sounding from the piano player.

'Maybe we'll do Driftwood's bank,' said Fraser softly after some time. 'It might be the only way.'

He leant back, lips inching into a grin.

Billy sipped his drink and scowled. He proffered Fraser unspoken curses, hated the man more with each passing minute. He was terrified too. He ached both from the slap he'd been given but also by his want to escape. Staying with Fraser, maybe even a few days more, might see them both flung headlong towards some inescapable disaster.

Ride away, Billy intoned silently. *Goddamn it, do it soon.* He eyed Fraser with a scathing glare. *No, Fraser, I won't cross any more goddamn miles with a mad bastard like you!*

Fraser contemplated too. He dropped his drained glass to the raised section's floorboard, clamped his eyes shut and pulled down his hat brim to shade his eyes.

Whatever dollars we make, he ruminated, *they're mine alone.* He opened his eyes briefly to lock Hall with a piercing look. *You'll die, Billy boy, between this night and Mexico!*

Jeb, departing the livery barn at 11.30 p.m., progressed along the now deserted and virtually silent boardwalk.

In his wake, Sam and TJ stood together in the barn's flung-open doors. Sam mused on the town's quietness too.

Apart from the sporadic night barks of dogs, or lock chains rattling when the wind gusts quickened, Driftwood seemed a haven of stillness in that cold plain's darkness. Sam brimmed with hope. Sullivan's gun exploits, he felt sure, had driven the thugs out for good. He stared intently at TJ now. That she'd bothered with a dress shocked him to the core; her lingering stares at Sullivan during dinner caused Sam rising disquiet.

'Jeb's a man what attracts trouble,' he growled with a nod. 'So far he's coped OK, but things might change!'

'Why'd you want him as sheriff, then?' TJ retorted truculently. 'What good's a sheriff if he don't stay alive?'

'He ain't afraid to face anyone. That's what we need in a sheriff,' Sam shrugged. 'God willing, he'll stay alive long enough to rid Driftwood of any scum.'

TJ's eyes widened and with a flushed complexion she spluttered, 'What if he doesn't? What if he's killed, damn it!'

'Sheriffs need to face down trouble,' growled Sam. 'If they die doing it that's how it is!'

'You don't care about Jeb,' she howled, unable to hide the anguish she felt. 'All this concern and kindness to the man was just about getting him to accept the badge?'

Sam nodded. 'That's about the score of it!'

Her emotions in a maelstrom now, TJ hurled herself onto the street. She yearned and feared for Sullivan with an intensity that hurt. That all too brief kiss in the shack, leaving her dizzy with wanting, also gave her the certainty they were destined to be together. But not with his wearing of a law badge in town. She'd found the man she dreamed of and wouldn't lose him for a sheriff's wage paid by people who didn't give a damn if he lived or died.

'I'll tell Jeb of your scheming,' she snarled. 'I'll make him see sense . . . I'll tell him to go away and stay safe.'

She ran down the night street, ignoring her pa's cries.

'TJ,' he yelled, 'get back here. Goddamn it, he's a born badge-wearer and you can't change it. Damn, you can't change the man!'

'I can,' she whispered, fighting the tears welling in her eyes, 'I'll keep Jeb alive no matter what it takes!'

The Regency Palace Saloon had cleared. Right then, still twenty minutes till midnight, as Fraser and Hall maintained their quiet vigil on the saloon's raised section, only James Scott and two others occupied the long bar. Scott, slumped headfirst over his table, murmuring softly, was hardly aware as two other long-beards approached him.

'Say, Jim,' proffered one. 'We're set back to the hills. You want to ride along of us?'

Scott looked up through blood shot eyes.

'Hell no, boys,' he slurred, 'you go; I'll drive back later. I've got more drinking to do!'

As the two miners left, Scott chuckled. He reached for his whiskey but clutched at air. He slid off his chair then, to lie in a groaning heap on the floor.

Hartford cursed and resolved to make amends. He glanced anxiously at the raised section, praying Fraser and Hall would leave soon. With them out of the way, Hartford would assist James Scott to his wagon.

Fraser stood now, quaffed the contents of his glass and stepped easily down the steps to the long bar. Soon, Billy following, Fraser strode towards the batwings. He halted, though, perusing the floored James Scott.

'You got dollars, Mr Long-beard?'

'The dogs wouldn't risk it,' James Scott snorted. 'Hell, I took chances and got my dream.' He looked up through blood shot eyes and said, 'Three big ones.' He patted his coat front with a hand and sighed. 'I'm set back to the hills to get me some more!'

Fraser nodded, jabbed a hand at Billy and with that they both exited the saloon. Out on the boardwalk, getting gloves on against the now biting cold, Fraser watched as TJ bustled down the street pursued by her liveryman father. He dragged Billy back into the shadows, and they waited.

TJ, barely able to breathe, heard the shack door creak as it opened. She gasped as Jeb showed, then she did her best to smile.

Jeb, stunned at her appearance, growled testily, 'TJ – it isn't but any time since I left your place. What's the matter?'

'Please,' she returned tremulously, 'we need to talk.'

Jeb shaped his lips to answer but a pounding of footfalls and rasping breath stilled his words. When Sam Griffin showed in the road, the old man gasped for air then jabbed a hand at TJ.

'Get home,' he wheezed, 'don't bother Sullivan this way.'

'I will not,' she barked a reply. 'Damn it, I'm a grown woman, Pa, and I know what I'm doing.'

'So help me,' Sam growled, 'if I have to—'

'No,' she bellowed. 'You beat me for rudeness; you'll sure not do it for being kind to this man.'

'Kind,' said Sam edgily, 'what in hell does—'

'Enough, Pa,' she snapped. 'Driftwood's emptied of thugs. I intend to speak with Jeb and I'll be back at the livery in a while. Now, please, just go, I beg you.'

Sam threw a piercing look at Jeb before he cursed under his breath and strode up Main Street towards the horse barn. TJ turned to nod at Jeb. 'I'll be pleased to come in, Mr Sullivan.'

Jeb hesitated at first, but then eased the door further ajar. He said nothing then, just watched intently until she'd entered. With the door shut, Jeb's heart pounded.

CHAPTER TEN

As Sam Griffin disappeared back through the livery barn's doors, Fraser stepped out of the dark and gave a sigh.

'Will you just look at that,' he grunted, jabbing a hand at the shack. 'Now why'd you reckon the livery bitch has gone there at this hour?' He snorted now, hand hovering on his gun. He eyed Billy intently. 'I've still got unfinished business with this Sullivan. First . . . there's three thousand to collect!'

Billy gasped, appalled. 'Goddamn it, Jake. What you got—' He choked off as Fraser hauled up his gun and levelled it.

'Get in the saddle,' Fraser said, 'and then we ride.'

As they urged their mounts out of town, someone else eased out of the street's dark edge. For Auger, what he'd just heard shocked him. He hovered a moment, finally ducking back into the dark as the batwings creaked ajar. He watched then as Hartford helped James Scott exit.

Auger ran now. Hurtling along the alleyways, only breathing easy when he slid in through the unbolted window of his home. As he scrambled into bed, Hartford finally got Scott onto his wagon.

Picking up the team's reins, sobered by the cold, Scott growled, 'Thanks. I'll be seeing you.' He flicked the gear and got the wagon trundling along Main Street and onto the plains.

Hartford, setting back to the saloon, mused intently as he went. He wondered about the nugget and what dollars he'd be offered for it at the bank.

Later, as Driftwood settled and the last lamplight flickered out, Hartford slid into the bed he'd inhabited alone since his wife chose separate sleeping arrangements.

'Another quiet night,' he mumbled as he closed his eyes. 'Maybe things have turned the corner.' He tingled with anticipation as he mused on Jeb Sullivan. If that man stayed in Driftwood and took the sheriff's badge, things might change. His last thought before sleep took him was of the nugget. He dreamt then of profit!

'You've had all evening to say stuff,' Jeb said pointedly as he sat, facing TJ across the shack's pine table. Yet you choose now and get your pa mad by doing it.'

'I didn't know before,' she snapped, 'not until Pa said so after you'd left the livery.'

'Said what?'

'How'd he'd drawn you like a fish on a hook.' Her eyes flashed indignant. 'He tricked you. All his sweet words were to get you to take the sheriff's badge.'

Jeb sighed. 'TJ, your pa's been upfront and honest enough. He near begged me to be law here in Driftwood.'

She looked confused. 'Did you know he and no other would care . . . so long as you kill thugs? You get yourself dead doing it, none would mourn!'

Jeb shrugged. 'That's how it is with law jobs,' he said

softly. 'You're expendable.' He stood now, looking vexed. 'I didn't accept the sheriff's badge on account of people being nice to me, TJ. I took it because—'

She lurched out of her seat, crossed to him quickly and dragged him to his feet. She threw her arms about him then and drew him into a passionate, lingering kiss.

'Don't do it,' she gasped when they broke away. 'If you feel anything for me you'll not let them kill you!'

He kissed her gently on the forehead before saying hoarsely, 'I took the badge because I wanted to stay close to you.'

Passion flamed between them. Nothing in the world could have stilled it. In time, locked in each other's arms on the bed, TJ stared longingly into his eyes.

'I love you, Jeb Sullivan.'

'What about me being sheriff?'

'If that's what it takes to keep you here.' She smothered him with kisses. 'Now I've found you I'll not lose you.'

Jeb shook his head. 'What d'you—'

'I'll raise a heck of deputies to keep you safe,' she said with an intensity that made Jeb shudder. 'I won't find my man then lose him.'

In time, as Jeb's outstretched hand doused the lamp, darkness curtained their love.

CHAPTER ELEVEN

In the face of another night's whipping wind, Jake Fraser and Billy Hall sat their mounts on the plains. Right then, a few miles to the north of Driftwood, they sought some shelter by a clump of dogwood trees.

Billy seethed with disquiet. God alive, he mused, depressed, to rob the drunken miner on his route back to the hills was an act of despicable evil. The man had risked life and limb to garner the nuggets with which he earned his pay and Fraser intended to take it all and leave the gold-digger destitute.

'Goddamn it,' Billy wailed in abhorrence now, 'He can't defend himself. I say we let the old miner alone!'

Fraser's sigh came layered with simmering rage. 'Keep pushing at me, boy,' he growled, 'you'll sure get sorry on it.'

Billy was about to protest but the clattering rattle of the approaching wagon intervened. When the vehicle halted with a jolt, the two mules pulling it baying loudly, a voice sounded.

'Say what?' James Scott hollered, 'Who's goddamn out there?'

'Just us,' yelled Fraser, urging his horse on, 'You know me, Long-beard?'

Scott did. Drunk and floored as he'd been in the saloon he recalled Fraser standing over him and asking about his money. Scott shook his head. He'd always steered clear of the Circle C hawker before, wary of the tales that circulated about town.

'You're a distance from Circle C land,' Scott grunted now. 'I need to get back to the hills. It's been a long, tough day!'

'Yeah,' returned Fraser, 'ain't that a fact?' He edged his horse closer, got the beast alongside the wagon and then leaned out of the saddle to set his mouth against James Scott's ear. 'Thing is, Long-beard,' he hissed, 'we're hawkers about here now and there's a toll to pay!'

Scott's eyes widened and he grunted tetchily, 'This is open prairie; it's goddamn government land. A man can—'

He stopped short as Fraser's gun jabbed at his temple.

'Now,' Fraser snarled, 'don't be pressing of me!'

Scott gulped before muttering, 'How much – to let me by?'

Fraser smirked. 'Let's say three thousand.'

Scott lips parted and a second after he gasped, 'You're goddamn crazy. Listen, mister, I ain't never—' His indignant outburst was quelled as a blow slammed him off the wagon. An instant later, as he hit the earth with a pained howl, he battled to stand but Fraser, sliding out of the saddle, delivered his gun butt to Scott's skull.

'OK,' said Fraser, dragging the stunned miner onto his

back. He slid his Colt back to its holster, got the knife out of the back of his belt and pressed the blade to Scott's throat.

'Oh, please, God,' Scott gasped. 'Don't—'

He quieted as he felt Fraser's free hand searching inside his shirt. A moment later, with the bag of money taken away, Scott felt the knife blade lifted also. Scott sat up, rubbing a hand to the hurt on his head before saying plaintively, 'This ain't right. That's my hard-earned money and I want it back.'

Fraser sighed, shoved the cloth bag into his own shirt and then nodded at Billy. 'See, boy, what it is to live free and easy?' He launched forward again, slamming a boot into Scott, who was now on his knees. His kick hammered into Scott's jaw and drove him groaning flat onto his back again.

'Billy boy,' Fraser bellowed now. He proffered the knife. 'Get off that horse and over here now!'

'But, Jake,' howled Billy, 'I don't want—'

'Now!' roared Fraser. 'I won't tell you again!'

Billy, sliding out of the saddle, approached with hesitant steps.

James Scott, his face dressed with blood, managed to sit up. 'This ain't right,' he mumbled, 'I'm set back to Driftwood.' He suppressed a sob before muttering tremulously, 'I'll tell on this. You won't get away with it!'

Fraser attacked again. He bedded the gun before hammering the miner with a swingeing punch. With Scott on his back once more, Fraser shoved the knife towards Billy.

'Do it,' he growled. 'Take the blade and stab the bastard!'

Billy edged away. 'Hell, no, Jake,' he gasped. 'There

isn't a need. Dear God, this is goddamn wrong.'

'Stab him, you son of a bitch!' Fraser roared, his eyes demonic. 'Do it!'

Billy, inching his hand to his gun, felt now the want to kill. He ached to wipe this crazed man Fraser off the earth – to ensure others didn't suffer at the psychopath's hands. Trouble was, although he'd worn a sidearm since the age of sixteen, Billy had never drawn the Colt .41 in anger. Fear and indecision stilled him now. Finally, with a howl he turned heel and ran. He sprinted the distance to his horse, leapt into the saddle and dragged reins. Before he got the horse into a headlong sprint, he heard the sickening sound of a struggle. The last thing he heard before his own desperate yells drowned it was a protracted, pain-layered wail. Billy wept then as he rode; he knew what that cry meant!

You've killed another innocent, Billy inveighed. *I'll hang too, Jake Fraser, for your demented ways!*

Uncontrollable terror drove Billy now. He felt or thought nothing for his horse. He just needed persistent speed; he needed the beast to put as much distance between him and Fraser as it could. He forced the animal to maintain its unyielding gallop, the mare thundering over that night-blackened land until its lungs burst and its legs started to buckle. When the horse faltered, its pace slowing, the now discernible hoofbeats of another beast chilled Billy's heart. Fraser had followed him; he'd gotten close.

'Oh, God,' Billy screamed. He tried to force more speed, but his mount shuddered at the cusp of exhaustion. When her front legs plunged, her head dropping fast, Billy vaulted out of the saddle and slammed to earth.

He hit the hard ground with a groan, lying aching and winded. He heard the snorting efforts of a fast-halted mount, then a thud of boots on ground followed by Fraser's venom-hissed words.

'You'd run out on me, would you, bastard?'

'Please, Jake,' Billy gasped. 'I didn't—' His words cut off as one of Fraser's fists hammered down. With blood exploding from teeth and nose, Billy lay spreadeagled and helpless.

'By God, boy,' Fraser snarled, 'you're walking the thinnest line with me.'

A pressure settled about Billy's throat and he struggled to breathe. Soon, spluttering, he tried desperately to loosen Fraser's death hold. He couldn't; he felt life draining out of him when Fraser swapped his hand for a knife. With the cold blade pressed to his jugular, Billy begged for his life.

'Oh, Jeez, don't cut me.'

Suddenly the knife's pressure eased. A second later, though, a force hammered once more into Billy's head. Drifting in and out of consciousness, spluttering blood, Billy wept.

'You never,' Fraser was snarling now, 'fail me again!' He dragged Billy to his feet. In time, when Billy had recovered some, Fraser added, 'It's a profitable night.' He patted the bulge at his coat front and said, 'Add this to what I'll get off Sullivan and it'll be a good life in Tiahuanaco.'

'The miner,' Billy mumbled through bruised and bloated lips. 'Tell me you didn't—'

'Critter food,' said Fraser. 'He's dead!'

Billy's head slumped and he proffered an unspoken prayer for the slain miner. Begging the Lord for forgiveness then, Billy made a vow. He'd kill against his own morals and judgement: he'd end the life of Jake Fraser for the betterment of the world!

CHAPTER TWELVE

Jeb awoke with light streaming through the shack's bedroom window. He sat up, looked and listened for TJ but realized that she'd already left. He smiled. She'd opened all the curtains and built a fire in the hearth in the front room.

Later, washed and dressed, Jeb drank coffee and planned the day. First, he'd speak with Mayor Collins, accept the sheriff's post and get sworn in. After that, he'd take breakfast at Malone's Eat House. Building a cigarette, he inhaled the sweet, scented smoke with a feeling of contentment.

This feeling was quelled when his thoughts settled on Sam Griffin. TJ's overnight stay would rile the old man and the horse tender would likely raise a complaint. Still, Jeb reasoned, and as TJ pointed out, she was a grown woman who'd the right to choices.

Jeb mulled on his life, altered now. That botched robbery had brought him to Driftwood; TJ and the kindness of the town's citizens would keep him here. With his aimless, grief-stricken wanderings over, he just felt a renewed vigour for life that left him almost breathless. Or did TJ do that for him ... sparking his vitality and dispelling his despair?

In time, outside and stamping his smoke butt in the dust, Jeb seethed with certainty. Wearing the law badge in Driftwood, he'd head the movement to revive the settlement's fortunes. Yes, he felt certain about this. In time, with the help of Mayor Collins, Sam Griffin and Ralph Hartford, Jeb would steer the town back to the stability and prosperity it once enjoyed.

He set off, then, certain about something else too. In turning Driftwood around, he'd marry TJ Griffin. About that, he'd no doubts at all!

The plains' air was baking as Fraser and Billy angled their mounts down the approach road and into the Circle C quadrangle. This spring, it seemed, man and beast would both suffer. Right now, little more than a couple of hours after dawn, the world burned under a hellish fire-faced sun. Soon, in the centre of the yard, they both off-saddled; Fraser mused tetchily on Wade Lever whilst Billy winced against the injuries he'd received.

Soon, Billy lifting a hand, he traced the swelling to his lips and the scattered clots of caked-dry blood. He ached, too; pain in his chin whilst his head throbbed with an intensity that brought tears to his eyes.

'That was a tough old night,' growled Fraser. He eyed Billy intently. 'Cold as hell.' He shook his head now. 'As cold as Hades by night; hot as hell by day, eh?'

Billy stayed his tongue. His hatred for Fraser intensified now with each passing minute. Through those cold, dark hours after the beating, Billy toyed with the idea of just

riding away, whatever the cost. He hadn't, though, debili-
tated once more by worry and indecision and the toll he'd
exacted on his mount. They'd located the wearied beast
nearby; a few hours' standing meant she'd recovered
some. She'd suffered bad, though, and would need careful
handling for the days that followed if she wasn't to be
damaged beyond hope.

Billy took his horse's reins now and began to lead the
beast towards the stabling block. Then he halted, watching
bemused as Wade Lever and six ranch-hands stepped out
of a barn and arranged themselves against a corral's bars.

'Would you take a look at that,' growled Fraser, shaking
his head. 'Now, why'd they be hovering about here, d'you
reckon?'

Billy gasped. Lever's appearance made panic rise as bile
but right then his bitterness toward Fraser dominated his
thinking.

'Howdy.' Lever proffered a wave. 'You had a good
night?'

'Get to hell, Lever,' snarled Fraser. He and Billy moved
into the stables where they worked on their horses before
easing them into stalls. In time, they stepped out to a
deserted yard.

'They've gone,' grunted Fraser. 'It's just as well for
them!'

Billy winced against the hurt all over his body and the
feeling of nausea in his guts. He'd readily forego breakfast, getting straight into his bunk and the sleep he craved.
However, he managed to steel himself to eat, knowing he
needed the food to keep up his strength.

Before long, they were seated at one of the chuck
house's long tables, plates laden with bacon and beans

from a frowning Meredith Lilley.

'Say, kid,' Meredith drawled, staring intently at Billy's swollen, bruised face, 'how'd you get beat up so?'

'The fool fell off his horse,' proffered Fraser, grabbing a fork and starting to eat.

Meredith, his eyes sparking with disbelief, shrugged and then muttered to Billy, 'When your meal's done, you'll stay. I'll fix you up some.'

Billy returned a nod and started to eat. In time, with Fraser building a smoke, Meredith motioned Billy to the rear of the hut. Over the minutes that followed, the chuck man tended Billy's injuries. He'd just finished, dropping a rag into the now blood-tainted water, when footsteps sounded on the hut's worn boards.

Wade Lever, a few steps ahead of the six ranch-hands, moved into the chuck house. Worryingly, each of them brandished a rifle that they soon levelled in Fraser's direction.

'On your feet,' Lever snarled, jabbing a hand. 'It's time I acted to put you two right on some things!'

Fraser's eyes sparked with fury whilst his right hand inched down to his strapped-on Colt. 'Get to hell,' he snarled. 'I said what'd occur if you kept pressing at me!'

Lever smirked. 'And I said what I'd do if I found you'd deserted your posts. Didn't you reckon I'd check on you again? I had my boys here scanning about the herd last midnight and hell . . . you boys weren't there!'

Fraser stood now, hand still on his gun butt. 'You're a goddamn liar,' he barked. 'We minded them beeves. Hell, you checked us the night before and saw it to be so!'

'It weren't so last night,' Lever drawled with a nod. 'Fact is, I figured to ride into Driftwood and catch you both but

I let that pass. You left the herd and that's good enough for me!'

Fraser laughed contemptuously. 'Good enough for you, son of a bitch? You're a two-bit hireling; you ain't a cattle boss.'

'When Seth Lomas is away,' said Lever, his words steady, 'I've full authority over men. That includes scum like you two.'

A taut silence ensued – a tensioned-layered hiatus through which Fraser's hand twitched at his gun butt and the six armed ranch-hands slid fingers to triggers. Fraser, knowing he couldn't shoot down half a dozen rifle-levelled foes, finally buckled. He inched his hand off the Colt and sighed deeply. 'What now, Lever?'

One of the ranch-hands delivered the answer. He strode forward, turned the rifle in his hold and slammed the butt into Fraser's guts. On his knees and groaning, Fraser was then dragged to the door.

'The barn,' Lever barked. He glared at Billy. 'You too, kid!'

'Don't beat this boy,' snapped Meredith. 'He's hurt enough.'

Lever's eyes sparked but then he nodded. 'I ain't got an issue with you, kid. You won't get harmed. Still, I'd want you to witness what happens to deserters so you'll know for the future.'

Inside the barn, with Fraser's duster and shirt dragged off, two men lashed his hands to a wagon wheel set upright against the rear wall. Billy gasped as the bag of Scott's money dropped to the floor. His eyes widened with disbelief then, as one of the ranch-hands picked up the bag and tossed it unchecked at him.

'You keep it till we're finished with the son of a bitch!'

Billy acted fast. He shoved the moneybag inside his own shirt and then he watched, trembling and sweating with fear. He'd heard Lever's assurance he wouldn't be hurt but disquiet still gripped him.

A sickening crack of noise made Billy jump and he watched, aghast, as Lever tested a bullwhip. When the brand foreman had readied his arm enough, he addressed his tethered victim.

'It pains me, this,' Lever said, 'but it'll pain you more!'

He didn't hold back. Sixteen grievous hits he applied to Fraser, the man's flesh shredded and bloodied when Lever desisted from the beating. Fraser had held out for the first few whip bites, but the pain became unbearable and finally he'd howled and screamed. He'd begged but still the biting scourge of the whip's end lashed into his skin. When it ended, Fraser sagging at his bounds and whimpering, Lever anchored Billy with a scathing glare.

'You're lucky, boy. Get away from the likes of Fraser. If you work another brand you stay loyal and do your duty!' He dropped the whip and jabbed a hand at Fraser. 'Get that bastard cleaned up and both of you off the Circle C. We see you again, you're both goddamn dead!'

It was two hours later that a groaning Fraser sat uneasily in his saddle whilst Billy guided both their mounts out of the Circle C yard.

'Get out of Kansas,' bellowed Lever as other ranch-hands laughed and guffawed. 'You goddamn pair of mollies!'

Billy cast a glance at the broken, beaten form of Jake Fraser and saw a tyrant brought to heel. This would change the psychopath, Billy felt sure.

'Let's head for Mexico,' he said then, determined to execute his escape that very night.

Fraser, his eyes tear-reddened but wide and full of fury, mouthed back, 'I go nowhere till the job's done.' His head slumped but he muttered softly as they rode, 'They all die!'

They came into Driftwood's branch of the Kansas State Bank just moments apart, both looking shifty. Ralph Hartford, jabbing a hand at Auger, urged the kid to seek service first. This Aaron did, moving to the counter and shoving money through the grille.

The teller, who'd seen James Scott proffer the boy a dollar the day before, shook his head. 'You got the earning way about you, boy!'

Aaron shrugged. 'It's all legal, mister.'

The teller sighed, logged the money in the book and noted Auger's impressive tally. Thirty-six dollars for a halfwit without employment was not bad going. When Auger left, Hartford plunged a hand into his pocket and shoved the gold nugget through.

The teller's eyes widened then he yelled, 'It's gold!'

Ralph, glancing edgily about and noting the jail's open door, glared fiercely at the teller, then hissed, 'Keep it goddamn quiet! I don't want my business told to all!'

The teller, shrugging, unperturbed, vacated the space behind the grille and Albert Lloyd quickly replaced him. Lloyd, thin and grim-faced, eyed the nugget before picking it up. He stared questioningly at Hartford before he walked off.

'What the hell—'

Lloyd halted near his office door and glared back. 'It needs to be weighed. You'll have to wait!'

So Hartford did, pacing the bank's polished wood floor and grumbling. It seemed an age before Lloyd reappeared and Hartford hurried to the grille.

'Well – goddamn it, how much?'

Lloyd's sombre countenance didn't alter. 'One hundred and sixty-six dollars. . . . Do you mind verifying how you acquired it?'

Ralph bristled, annoyed. 'What the hell does it matter?' His ire quelled fast then, when he considered the profit. 'It's payment for bar debt. Some men pay in money; some don't!'

Lloyd looked ready to protest but he kept quiet. He wrote out a sale docket and slid it through the grille with a pen. 'If you'd sign and date.' Soon, he pushed dollar notes through, which Ralph collected gratefully before exiting fast.

'Scott gave him that nugget,' the teller said. 'Got to be.'

Lloyd nodded and strolled back to his office. He detested gold – it brought out the worst in people, including him. In time, the nugget in a safe, he sank into his seat and groaned. He turned his attention to the letter to the bank's head office in Dodge City. *Close Driftwood's branch of the bank*, he suggested, *owing to a spate of killing in the town.* As far as Albert Lloyd was concerned, this settlement was a lost cause and nothing could save it!

CHAPTER THIRTEEN

Billy cursed his own weakness as they rode. He'd gotten his chance to escape Fraser's insidious grip but he just couldn't take it. He looked to his left, watched Fraser's slumped form in the saddle whilst the man howled with each step his horse made.

You've been broken, Billy ruminated now. *They near killed you and you've been brought to your knees, you scum!*

Billy recalled Fraser's pitiful wails in that barn. They were gut-wrenching screams; howls from the very core of a man's personal hell. Although he hated Fraser with a passion now, Billy struggled not to feel sympathy for the son-of-a-bitch wretch!

There was something more. That man, whip-lashed and hurt bad, would surely die if Billy abandoned him. Maybe Fraser deserved such a fate, Billy mulled, but that didn't salve his mind. Billy just knew he couldn't do it. He couldn't abandon a helpless man, no matter that man's vile and violent pedigree.

They rode on through, across those sweltering flatland miles, only halting when Billy sighted a spiral of smoke ahead. Moving on again, a log hut lifted out of the long

89

grass distance.

Close by that house, Billy bellowed out, 'Hi there. I've a sick man aside me. I need help!'

The hut's door opened and the man that showed, a shotgun to hand, growled, 'Who needs help? Who the hell are you?'

'My name's Hall,' Billy proffered naively. 'Fraser here is hurt. He took a hell of a beating a few hours since!'

The man with the shotgun stepped off the hut's veranda. Edging forward, the double barrel levelled, he got to the side of Fraser's horse and eyed the slumped posture of the man in the saddle. He looked intently at Billy.

'I'm not sure,' he grunted, 'I don't usually—' He broke off, as Fraser crashed out of the saddle with a groan. Dropping the shotgun, the man gathered Fraser in his stout arms and cushioned his fall. 'Help me,' he said decisively to Billy. 'We'll get him into a bed and I'll look at his wounds.'

Much later, Fraser asleep with his back bathed and bandaged, the hut's owner joined Billy in the kitchen.

'He's been goddamn scourged,' the man growled. 'I saw the same during the war. Deserters got it . . . mostly they didn't live from their wounds.' He dropped into a chair with a sigh. 'He'll live, with rest, good food and me tending those scars.' He sighed then. 'I'm Donald Highwood – ex-bison man.' He gave a smile. 'That's what got me this place. It ain't much – a few chickens and pigs – but a site to farm a bit.'

Billy nodded. 'I'd like the same one day. I'd work it with a wife and have young ones running outside.'

'Your buddy in there,' said Highwood with a frown. 'He

90

kept raving stuff about money. He's running a fever.' His look was searching now. 'You ain't wanted or anything like that, are you?'

Billy paled but kept his words steady. 'He's not my buddy, Mr Highwood. I'm no danger to anyone!' He dragged out the bag of money from his shirt and removed twenty dollars. Setting the banknote on the table, he said, 'That's for lodging and care of Fraser.'

'Good,' Highwood said, pocketing the offer and then getting to his feet. 'I'll get some grub on.'

As Highwood fashioned the meal, Billy stepped out to the porch and dropped onto a rocking chair. He stared wistfully into the long grass distance, cursing softly. He'd mulled the perils of staying close to Fraser enough times but still he remained. He didn't need to be told why. Deep down, Billy recognized the host of positive attributes ascribed him by his parents – a caring nature; an innate kindness and a sanctity for life. All these would need to guide his actions from this point on. His one failure – letting Reece persuade him into Fraser's gang – could still be Billy's ruin but he just prayed he could make amends. Even at this critical juncture, though, kindness affected his thinking. He'd stay with Fraser until that man recovered, he decided, and at that point he would ride away.

Fraser'll be altered, Billy willed now. *Perhaps that whipping beat the evil out of him!*

People do change, Billy reasoned, even men as vicious and cruel as Jake Fraser. As for the murder of James Scott – Billy didn't dare think about that. The enormity of that crime was just too much to bear.

Billy mused now on his future. When he did finally ride, he'd set north to fashion his new life alone.

As Billy planned, Fraser's eyes opened. He bit at the sheets, battling the hurt raging across his back. He glanced about then, confused. Where he was or how long he'd been there he didn't know. He was certain of one thing, though: when his wounds healed, he'd enact a hurricane of vengeance. These heat-parched plains would colour red with blood!

For Jeb, the following hours passed busily. Sworn in by Mayor Collins, he now sported a sheriff's badge and spent time getting used to the jail. He studied it all – the cell-block and ammunition rack; the safe with its thousand-dollar contents, presumably for payment of a bounty should any man have ground to claim some. By mid-afternoon, he joined Collins and some locals to watch the burials of Corrigan, Hayes and Taylor.

It was a muted affair, the dead not missed or mourned by anyone. With no man of faith to preside over the ceremony, Mayor Collins did it.

'Ashes to ashes,' he muttered, 'in hope of resurrection and eternal life. . . .' He watched then, as the trio of sheet-swathed corpses, lowered by rope, settled into a pit outside of town. He said sourly then, 'If they avoid hell they'll be lucky!'

As Waverley and his son shovelled soil over the interred dead and locals drifted away, only Jeb and the mayor held their ground.

'With those thugs under earth,' grunted Collins, 'I'm hoping Driftwood might quieten some.' He shrugged. 'Word is that Seth Lomas at the Circle C had a surprise beef order come in. He's set to Dodge City with most of his crew.'

Jeb nodded. 'Not Jake Fraser and Billy Hall, though.'

'Perhaps,' retorted the mayor, his words edged with hope, 'those two will think twice afore tackling you, Sheriff Sullivan.'

'The Circle C,' Jeb said edgily, 'that cattle drive to Dodge. I guess you heard about it from Auger?'

'Sort of. I heard two women talking.' The mayor sighed. 'Auger told those ladies, and I heard it from them.'

Jeb frowned. 'I spoke with that boy yesterday. I warned him off all this gossiping. It'll get him into trouble, sure enough.'

Collins nodded. 'But God darn it, he's good at it.' The mayor sighed. 'Auger seems to know about stuff before it's even happened.' His look was edgy now. 'Like the issue of a deputy!'

'A deputy?' Jeb's countenance clouded. 'You couldn't recruit a sheriff until I came. Who in hell do you plan to get as deputy?'

'Who do *I* plan? I thought it was you who wanted an assistant, Sullivan – leastways that's what I heard?'

Jeb swallowed down his anger. 'It'll be TJ's doing,' he grunted, 'and put about town by Auger.' Jeb shook his head and touched a hand to the Colt strapped at his leg. 'This is my assistant. I'm fine on my own right about now!'

Collins smiled. 'That's OK, then. Why not lock Auger in the cells a while? That might shock his tongue still!'

Parting then, Jeb set to the jail whilst Collins headed home.

Auger, who'd watched the burial from a distance, sat on the boardwalk and tracked Sullivan's walk. When the new sheriff entered the jail, he stood and yawned. He'd slept little the previous night, tossing and turning, worrying incessantly over the fate of his friend James Scott.

Aaron settled upon a resolution now. He'd saddle the pinto in his pa's barn and then ride out to the Sabre Hills. He'd make sure James Scott was OK. Maybe, Auger reasoned as he walked to his home, Scott would be so impressed with Aaron's compassionate concern he'd proffer a small reward.

In time, astride the pinto just outside of town, he got the mare moving with heels and yells.

He planned as he rode through the day's wilting heat. He'd keep making profit, peddling any stories for dollars until his savings swelled. He'd set to Dodge City then. Heck, there'd be gossip enough amongst that city's massive populace to make someone very, very rich. People paid to hear tales . . . it didn't matter if they were true or not!

CHAPTER FOURTEEN

TJ showed in the law office just before midday. She held a plate draped with a cloth. She set this down and took off the cloth, revealing a meal of bacon, beans and biscuits.

'A snack,' she said with a smile. 'I guessed you'd be busy; a sheriff needs to keep his strength up!'

Jeb nodded, battling the urge to confront her over the matter of a deputy. He held his tongue, though. Her hapless attempts to keep him safe were a minor consideration, given everything else that had occurred since he'd arrived in Driftwood. Besides, it would seem churlish, given she'd made him this meal. He got a fork out of one of the desk drawers and soon devoured the offering. With the cleared plate set aside, he watched as she poured coffee out of the pot into a mug. She placed this on the desk and watched intently as he built a smoke. As he lit the cigarette and inhaled, she moved behind him, wrapped her arms about his neck and snuggled her head against his.

'Last night,' she whispered into his ear, 'I was so happy!'

'Is your pa happy too?'

She pulled back, stalked around the desk and faced him with fiery eyes. 'He's said little and he won't either. Hell, he wanted me to find a man and now I have!' She sighed. 'It's fate, Jeb Sullivan, that brought you to me.'

'Fate?' Jeb's eyes sparked with hurt. 'That's either a helpful servant or the cruellest master!'

'Your wife and boy,' she intoned softly then. 'Was that meant to happen ... hell, no! My ma neither. It just happens. In a land of guns, people die.' Her face reddened with ire. 'If we'll tame this land, God only knows, but until we do, some live whilst others won't. Those that survive keep on living. In my mind, fate only brings good things. It was fate you married your wife and you shared your boy for a few years at least. It was fate I had my ma right up to the point a scum dog shot her.'

She fell silent and Jeb grunted, 'Are you finished, missy?'

'It was fate that brought you to Driftwood,' she raged on again, 'but I couldn't see it at first. Fate will keep you here and us together.' She moved to the jail door. 'Dinner's 8 p.m., Mr Jeb Sullivan, if you're minded to attend?'

He nodded and ached for her. 'And you, TJ, are you minded to pay me another midnight visit?'

'Damn you,' she cursed as she plunged outside. She gasped as she ran, willing hours to pass so she'd be in his arms again. When she reached the livery doors, she stared back at the jail. 'Wild horses,' she said with certainty, 'won't keep us apart!'

Circling buzzards drew Auger in. Slowing his horse, he

stared, appalled at the unsettling scene ahead. Scavengers mauled a body – a squawking cover of birds ripping at flesh whilst a wolf closed in, snarling for room. Aaron, retching violently, sprayed vomit to earth. When his guts settled, he noted the stilled wagon with the two mules bucking, agitated in the staves.

Regaining composure he acted quickly now. He grabbed the rifle out of its saddle sheath, fumbled a cartridge into the breach and then took a trembling aim. A second later, as the gun bucked in his grip, he watched, satisfied, as one of those abhorrent buzzards crashed dead to earth. As the other birds took flight and that wolf sprinted into retreat, Aaron slid out of the saddle and took tentative steps forward.

Before long, suppressing a sob, Auger gazed appalled at James Scott's ravaged corpse. The miner, spreadeagled on his back, lacked eyes to appraise anything whilst his clothes hung as rags about his ripped and gored flesh. Where the man's chest and guts met, a puncture point was clearly visible, coated now by a caulk of dried, blackened blood.

'Oh, God!' Auger lurched away. He got to his horse, sheathed the rifle and then he waited. Fraser and Hall; that three thousand dollars – it was simple enough: robbery and murder. Where one man profits another yearns. He'd set back to Driftwood to raise a hue and cry.

A sudden clattering noise made him pause. He scanned frantically about, then watched appalled as a wagon halted in a swathe of dust. Aaron's guts turned. The two men on the wagon's cross-seat both eyed him with looks of fury.

'Jesus H Christ,' snarled the one at the reins, throwing

a fast look at the corpse. 'You've killed Scott?'

The other man levelled a rifle and spat, 'Hands high, boy; we're taking you in for murder.'

Auger, face paled, his whole body trembling, shook his head. 'I didn't . . . I mean, hell, I wouldn't. . . .'

'See,' barked the man with the rifle. 'He can't get the words out he's so scared he's been caught.'

'It's lucky we rode by,' growled the other, dropping the reins. 'Scott didn't get back last night and we set to Driftwood to find him. Hell, we find his corpse and his killer instead!'

Aaron, his legs buckling, battled not to faint. He grabbed for the saddlehorn, trying desperately to stay upright. When he'd quelled the dizziness, panic swelled as bile and he spluttered, 'I didn't. . . . Oh, God, please I didn't—'

The crack of that levelled Winchester rent the baked plains' silence and Aaron crashed to ground. He slammed to the hard, dry earth but got to his feet fast again as a slug bit soil. Into the saddle then, he drove his horse with heels and desperate screams. Forcing his mount to the north, he wept as he rode. The world shattered into a million pieces. He'd be wanted for murder and have to ride out his days pursued like a hunted animal!

Fraser sat up with a grunt. His back still ached, but he managed to ease himself out of the bed. He sighted his shirt, draped over a chair. With this on, he scanned the room. He noted the open door and bellowed. 'Hall, where are you?'

Billy soon showed with astonishment on his face.

'Jake,' he gasped, 'I didn't reckon you'd be OK so quick.'

Fraser's own countenance clouded. 'Where goddamn are we?'

'A half-day's ride north of the Circle C.' Billy shrugged. 'We've struck lucky. A man called Highwood owns this farm. He says you need rest . . . time for those wounds to heal.'

Fraser spat at the boards then growled, 'We ain't got time. It's but days till Lomas gets back from Dodge. I want stuff done by then.' He jabbed a hand. 'We'll ride out!'

Billy's guts turned. 'But, Jake,' he protested, 'We can't—'

'Enough,' Fraser growled. He grabbed his gun-belt off a table and strapped it on. 'I want my money and I want my revenge. First we go after Wade Lever and those bastards at the Circle C!' He glared about the room, his jaw muscles twitching. 'Speaking of money – where's my bag of dollars?'

Billy, sliding the bag out of his shirt, passed it over.

Fraser, with a curt nod, shoved the bag into his own shirt and said curtly, 'I'll settle things with this man Highwood.'

'I've already done it,' said Billy with a shrug. 'I gave him twenty dollars for looking after us.'

Fraser's eyes blazed. 'You did goddamn what?' He stepped forward and proffered a sharp slap to Billy's face. 'You dog. Never give away my money, you hear!'

Billy battled the swell of rage and despair. He rubbed a hand to the sting at his jaw and said bitterly, 'That's it. I'm riding out alone. I've taken beatings enough from you.'

He turned to leave but halted as a click of a gun's hammer sounded. Inching about, he stared into the muzzle of Fraser's levelled Colt.

'You're going nowhere, Billy boy, excepting to hell if you give me any more lip.' Fraser's eyes sparked with fury. 'By Christ I'll teach you better than to back-chat me!'

Billy's heart sank. Fraser's beating hadn't altered the man at all. Just as evil and malicious as he'd always been, he was mobile once more and set towards more crime.

'What now, Jake?' Billy growled, depressed. 'You planning to keep that Colt aimed at your partner?'

Fraser smirked. 'I ain't sure, Billy boy. You're hellish uppity and talking of riding out on me. What's a feller to do?'

'I've stood by you,' Billy bellowed, his anger overriding his worry now. 'Damn it. I could have ridden when you were dead in the saddle after that whipping. I stayed; I brought you to here where Highwood tended your wounds.'

Fraser stayed quiet a moment before he nodded and slid his Colt to its holster. 'Right you was, Billy boy.' He proffered a wink. 'I need you, Billy boy. We'll ride to Tiahuanaco where we'll have equal shares and live out our lives like kings!'

'Yeah,' said Billy softly, cursing against the deceit and charade of it all.

Fraser moved forward then and slid Billy's pistol out of the holster on his right leg. He tossed gun to floor, saying with a wink, 'Get moving. You'll saddle the horses.'

Billy hesitated a moment but then he walked. When he moved into the hut's kitchen, Highwood rose from a seat at the table.

'It's unbelievable,' said the farmer with a nod at Fraser who appeared in the bedroom's doorway. 'You've an ox's constitution to get over a whipping so quick, Mr Fraser.'

Fraser's vexed look preceded a sigh. 'Well, Highwood, it'll take more than a beating to keep me down.' He jabbed out a hand. 'Billy boy says you've gotten twenty dollars of my money?'

Highwood shrugged. 'That's right. I'm not wealthy; I can't afford to take guests without some help!'

Fraser frowned. 'Well, that's grand. Fact is we're setting out.' He glared at Billy. 'Get the horses saddled and bring both rifles in here.' He turned to Highwood then. 'You got any pieces out in that barn?'

'No,' Highwood nodded at the shotgun propped against a wall, 'only that thing.'

'Don't try anything stupid,' Fraser snarled at Billy then. 'Just saddle those mounts, bring the guns and I'll stay here with Highwood.' He dragged up his Colt and jabbed it at the farmer. 'You're life's resting on Billy being sensible.'

Billy hesitated but then he moved. Out on the porch, he jumped down to the yard and set to the barn. Soon, with both horses saddled and ready, he slid his rifle from its sheath and grabbed Fraser's Carbine. When he got back to the hut, he set both guns on the kitchen table.

'Good,' Fraser growled. He jabbed with his Colt again. 'Wait with the horses, Billy boy!'

Billy shook his head. 'But, goddamn it I don't—' He howled as Fraser stepped the distance and slapped out again.

'Get to the horses, boy!'

Billy, swallowing back his tears, exited to the barn. With both animals led outside, he waited and prayed.

In the hut, Fraser and Highwood shared glares over the table.

'I've treated your wounds with poultice,' Highwood

101

proffered at length. 'I'll put some in a bag and your partner there can apply it. It'll aid the mend.'

Fraser shook his head. 'Is it any good on bullet holes?'

Highwood's eyes widened. 'Look, mister, I don't—' His words choked off as Fraser flat-palmed the Colt's hammer and sent a bullet smashing into the farmer's chest. As the slug slammed into flesh and bone, Highwood staggered backward, only halting when he met the shack's wall. He groaned, clutched hands to the gaping fissure, then, eyes rolling, he slid to floor. He sat, head slumped, a blood trail snaking down the wall above his head.

'That poultice ain't much good if you're dead, neither,' said Fraser with a grunt. He re-holstered the Colt, stepped forward and rifled through the dead farmer's pockets. With money found, he lifted his rifle off the table and stepped fast outside.

Billy, calming the horses, felt disgust as Fraser showed.

'Damn it,' he bellowed, 'I take it you just shot Highwood?'

'What's it to you?' Fraser snarled, 'He's just some hick sodbuster when it's said and done!'

'You stinking son of a bitch,' Billy bellowed, consumed with fury. 'Since the cursed day I met you all you've done is beat, bully and kill. I'll swing for the blood you've spilt.'

Fraser's look was unreadable. When Billy gradually calmed, the killer said softly, 'You'll swing lessen you stay with me into Mexico. You try to ride alone, you're dead for sure.' He chuckled. 'I mean, you ain't got a gun, have you?'

He slid his rifle to its saddle sheath and got onto his horse. He waited for Billy to mount before grunting, 'You ride ahead; I'll see what you're up to.'

In time, as they eased their mounts onto the plains,

both mused silently that the end drew close. In Fraser's mind it would be with dollars to hand and all those that had ailed him dead – including Billy Hall.

Billy just prayed for salvation. Whatever it took, he had to escape the demonic hold of Jake Fraser.

CHAPTER FIFTEEN

'We brought the body straight here,' gasped one of the miners as he addressed Jeb in the Driftwood jail. 'We got his goddamn corpse on our wagon. We've brought his mules too.'

Jeb, stepping outside, jumped down into the street and looked into the wagon's buckboard. Soon, others started to show, drawn by the commotion. When Collins appeared, he joined Jeb at the back of the wagon. He looked down, his face pale.

'James Scott. Dear God, this killing just isn't stopping.'

'That halfwit Auger done it,' one of the long-beards called from the jail doorway. 'We caught him knelt by Scott's corpse.'

Jeb shook his head. 'You said you'd found this dead feller a couple of hours ago on the prairie?'

The miner nodded. 'Yeah, just after Auger killed him.'

Jeb jabbed a hand at the cadaver. 'Jeez, look at the critter marks. This James Scott is so stiffened by time, it's likely he was killed sometime last night.'

The two miners' faces darkened. 'Goddamn,' growled one. 'I didn't think on that. I saw Auger and reckoned him the killer.'

The other nodded. 'I could've killed the boy. I blasted my rifle at him but I missed. The boy skedaddled then.'

'What was Aaron doing out on the prairie?' growled Collins now. 'He's always up to some kind of no good.'

'I don't know,' said Jeb with a sigh. 'But I aim to find out.' He soon did. After questioning both miners more in the jail, he set to the saloon to talk to Ralph Hartford. Later still, he interrogated Albert Lloyd at the town's bank. Finally, with dusk patterning Main Street with shadow, he updated Collins.

'It seems Scott struck gold and brought nuggets into town yesterday to cash in at the bank. He set to the saloon first, though, getting so drunk Auger helped him to make his deposit.'

'Auger was in the saloon too?'

'Yeah,' said Jeb with a nod. 'With his money to hand, Scott then set back to the saloon and he was still drinking past midnight when those two miners offered to accompany him back to the Sabre Hills. He declined and must've set back on his own. Between here and where they found the body, someone attacked him.'

'Auger had motive,' mused Collins. 'He knew Scott had money and the way Aaron lusts after dollars it would add up. Thing is, I've known Auger all his life. He wouldn't hurt a fly!'

'Hartford had motive too,' added Jeb. 'Lloyd at the bank said Hartford deposited a nugget himself yesterday. Hartford said someone gave it to him in lieu of bar debt – most likely James Scott. Yet, when I spoke to Hartford, he didn't mention that.'

Collins shrugged. 'I've known Ralph a heck of years

too. He wouldn't hurt anyone, neither!'

Jeb gave an agitated sigh. 'I pressed both those miners and Ralph Hartford about who else was in the saloon late last night but they all said there weren't anyone.'

Collins shrugged now. 'That's it, then. You've gotten two suspects – one in the saloon, the other now missing. I'll say with certainty, mind, Auger and Hartford aren't capable of murder.'

Jeb nodded. He'd felt certain as he questioned the saloon keeper and that pair of gold miners that things were being withheld, most likely in respect of the saloon's midnight occupants. He didn't say anything to Collins, though. It was just a hunch – a gut feeling that the person you're speaking too isn't being fully liberal with the truth. However, he couldn't prove it. As he mulled more, and with the mayor departing the jail now, in Main Street the two gold miners watched sombrely as Hank and Chris Waverley lugged Scott's body towards their property.

Soon, with both of them standing at the long counter of the Regency Palace, one whispered to Hartford, 'That sheriff pressed on who was in here when we left last night. We said four . . . us two, you Hartford and Scott. We didn't say on you-know-who?'

Hartford nodded grimly. He'd omitted to admit Fraser's presence in the Regency Palace also. The last thing he needed was a hoodlum like Fraser bearing a grudge.

'Listen,' he said edgily. 'I'd say a drifter blasted Scott and they're long gone. It's best to let sleeping dogs lie, eh?'

The two miners nodded and, drinks to hand, moved to a table. Hartford set to buffing glasses. He mused on

Sullivan's earlier questioning – this new sheriff possessed a manner that made even the innocent quake.

Hartford mused on his own culpability now. He'd served Scott extra drinks; he'd allowed the man to drink himself near senseless.

'God's sake,' he hissed. 'It ain't my fault Scott's dead.'

He repeated this a few times over the ensuing hours but his feeling of uneasiness he couldn't dislodge. He dwelled on the missing Auger then and felt genuine concern. The kid was somewhere out there on the vast evening plains and likely scared to death. What disquiet Hartford felt, Auger's would be a hundredfold.

'Come back, Aaron,' Hartford muttered softly, glancing at the batwings. 'We all know you didn't do it!'

'He didn't do it!' TJ screamed in the livery barn after Jeb told her. She launched forward, pummelling his chest with her fists. Jeb quickly stilled her rage. Taking her gently by the wrists, he clamped a kiss to her lips that settled her ire instantly. When Jeb stepped away, he gave sigh.

'I'm sure Auger didn't do it,' he said with a grunt. 'Scott died last night after leaving the saloon. Someone else was in the Regency Palace but it seems folk are too scared to tell me more than they have to!'

TJ nodded glumly. 'I'll say it if others lack the guts—'

'No, TJ!' Sam showed through a door and shook his head. 'We weren't there; it's not for us to guess. You'll keep quiet.'

She rounded on her pa, fire in her eyes. 'Aaron's out there, Pa. He's likely scared stupid he's branded a killer.'

'I heard,' returned Sam edgily. 'I've been listening.' He

eyed Jeb intently. 'I'd say you'll raise a posse . . . not to arrest Auger but to find that boy safe.'

Jeb nodded. 'I'll speak to Collins right away.' He went to leave but halted at the barn doors. 'Auger's pa, you'll—'

'I'll tell him,' returned Sam with a nod. 'It'll break old Mr Auger's heart but he needs to know.'

Jeb left then and TJ shaped to exit the barn too.

'You're going nowhere,' Sam said icily. 'You ain't got no place out there.'

TJ scowled but could see by her pa's harsh look he wouldn't brook dissension. Soon, the livery doors shut, they set by a back route towards the shack Auger shared with his father.

'It'll kill him,' Sam said. 'How will that man cope?'

TJ's thoughts focused on the likely killers: Jake Fraser and Billy Hall she felt certain were involved. But her pa had warned her: don't implicate dangerous people in anything. The risk of doing that was just too great. She worried about Jeb then. If she'd been on the posse, she'd ensure he'd stay safe.

'You'll stay right by my side,' Sam muttered as they closed on the Auger shack, 'until this killing spree is finished with.'

'But Jeb needs. . . .' She quieted, swallowed her anguish.

Sam held his own tongue. She'd spent all night at the shack and Sam knew what that meant. He cursed without words. The first time she'd shown close to a man and it had to be the new sheriff. Jeb Sullivan – a killing machine who faced death head on and attracted it, too. What good was he as a husband? TJ would marry one day and be widowed the next!

'I already said not to get too close to Sullivan,' he said to her softly now. 'He's not the sort to stay long.'

TJ maintained her brooding silence. It was too late for that. Her heart was lost to the man from Missouri. He'd never leave, and if he did they'd depart together. Their lives, irrevocably intertwined now, couldn't be parted. Not if TJ could do anything about it!

At Fraser's command, they'd halted. Now, on the fast-darkening dusk plains, they both listened. Hoofbeats drummed loud. A horse approached.

Fraser, dragging his rifle to hand, slid a cartridge into the bridge and cocked the gun. He levelled it then before bellowing, 'Stop, son of a bitch, or you're dead!'

The hoofbeats gradually stilled. A blur in the gloom hollered out now, 'Please, sir . . . I ain't holding a gun!'

Fraser lowered the rifle and shook his head. He recognized the voice instantly. He grunted, 'Boy, is that you?'

Auger's loud gasp preceded a tremulous, 'It's me, Auger.'

'Well, ride here slow and easy.'

Auger urged his horse forward, and soon he was staring, grim-faced and silent, at Fraser and Hall.

Fraser spat, 'What're you doing out here?'

Aaron crumpled. The shock of the last hours erupted into tears. Weeping, he spluttered, distressed, 'They say I murdered Scott. I found the body and then miners set by. They'll go to Driftwood; they'll get the sheriff after me!'

Fraser exploded with laughs. When they quelled he snorted, 'That's a damn!' He slapped a hand to a leg. 'This halfwit gets roped with the killing.'

Aaron stilled his tears, saying sourly, 'I didn't kill

anyone.' He wanted to say what he knew – to accuse Fraser of the evil act. Hell, he'd heard what they'd said on the late-night boardwalk. They'd wait for the drunken Scott to set out of town. Instead, shrugging, Auger said meekly, 'I don't rightly know what to do. I don't want to get hung!'

'You stay with us, boy,' returned Fraser with a wink. He cast a sly look at Hall. 'Ain't that right, Billy?'

'Yeah,' Billy grunted sourly, 'whatever you say.'

Fraser, edging his horse forward, reached for the rifle in Auger's saddle sheath. With that to hand, he tossed it to earth.

'Now,' he growled, 'we ride for the Circle C.'

They went at a canter, a couple of miles underfoot before Aaron settled his mount aside Billy's horse. Behind, some fifty feet or so, Fraser rode guard.

'What's likely to happen to me?' asked Aaron, throwing Billy a panicked look. 'I don't how I'll get out of this.'

Billy pinned Auger with a withering stare. 'Lessen someone tells the truth, you might hang.'

Auger stifled a howl. 'I didn't kill that miner.' He fixed Billy with a pleading gaze as he whispered, 'But you'd know that!'

Billy's eyes sparked. 'Listen,' he hissed, 'we're in a tight spot. I don't know what that crazy son of a bitch has got planned but I'd say it ain't good. We've got to get away from Fraser.'

Aaron nodded again. 'So he—'

'Yeah,' cut in Billy, 'he knifed Scott.'

'He's your partner,' rasped Auger. 'Why'd you—'

'Riding aside Fraser,' Billy grunted, 'means nothing. He's crazy; he's got guns and we don't. We've got to get away!'

Aaron nodded. He'd survive and he'd keep Hall alive

too. Billy Hall – the man who possessed evidence of Aaron's innocence.

I'll get through this, Aaron intoned as he rode. *And so help me I'll never tell tales again if I live to be a hundred!*

CHAPTER SIXTEEN

Just past 7 p.m. Ralph Hartford perused the crowd of local men now filling the Regency Palace Saloon. They'd been summoned, by two local youths who'd criss-crossed town to circulate word.

Behind the counter, Hartford watched it all and proffered a soft curse. The locals weren't for drinking and all his other customers had dispersed. The two miners had set back to the hills whilst the drifters had fled. All this talk of killing and posses wasn't good for trade. Frowning behind his bar, Ralph listened to the hubbub of voices then watched, vexed, as the mayor and Sullivan entered through the batwings.

Collins moved swiftly. Grabbing a chair, he stood on it and raised a hand for quiet. With a hush established, he nodded.

'Listen,' he said loudly, 'Aaron Auger's somewhere on that prairie. I need men willing to ride out and find the boy.'

A new burst of talking swelled. Auger, for all his busy-body ways, was popular. Men glanced at Jeb, rumours about his killing powers having swept about the settlement.

'Sheriff will ride along of us?' called out one middleager.

'Yes,' said Jeb. 'I want Auger brought back safe and well.' He studied the massed faces. 'You'll all know Scott is dead?'

'Yeah,' grunted one man. 'Whoever murdered that miner it weren't Auger. That boy ain't got such in him!'

Jeb nodded. 'It seems most think that way. Truth is, though, Auger was seen aside Scott's dead body today and I need to know why. That means finding Auger quickly and alive.'

'I'll help,' yelled a man with his arm held high. Others soon followed suit. Before long, Jeb counted twelve volunteers. Whilst the posse stayed, the remainder exited to their homes.

Jeb pointed at two of the volunteering men then. 'You fellers – I want a guard in town. I reckon that's best.'

Collins nodded at that. 'I'll be here as backup. With three of us I'd say that should be sufficient.'

Jeb sighed. 'OK . . . the rest of you, bring horses and guns and meet me outside the saloon in thirty minutes.'

As men filed out, Hartford got whiskey to glasses and set them on the counter.

'You'll find Auger,' Ralph said edgily. 'I'm sure of it.'

Jeb downed one of the whiskey shots before grunting, 'We'll try to find him. Finding who killed Scott will take time.' He pulled a coin from his jeans and slapped it onto the counter.

'Hell,' Hartford growled. He pointed to a room at the rear of the saloon. Inside there, with the door shut,

Hartford sighed, 'Scott settled his debt with a nugget. I plied him with whiskey. What a man drinks is his business.' He reddened in the face, uttering words layered with tension, 'They were in last night . . . Fraser and Hall.'

Jeb dropped a hand to the butt of his gun. 'And they knew Scott had a heck of money on him.'

Hartford shrugged. 'I can't say that. They spoke with him is all I can swear.' He thought back, recalling that point where Scott fell off his chair and had some sort of an exchange with the exiting Fraser. 'That Circle C thug talked to Scott but what got said I just don't know.'

Jeb looked piercingly at Collins then. 'My first stop will be the Circle C. I want to speak to these boys Fraser and Hall.'

'OK,' returned Collins, 'but be careful. I'd go as far as to say Fraser ain't right in the head!'

As Jeb stalked out of the room, Collins smiled. 'I'm grateful you spoke the truth, Ralph. I'd say Sullivan can start putting pieces together and get Auger safe!'

Hartford looked grim. He, like everyone else in town, just knew Auger didn't have it in him to kill. The murderer had to be Fraser. Right now, Ralph just hoped and prayed they'd find Aaron safe and bring Fraser to justice. If they didn't – if Fraser evaded prosecution – and the Circle C hawker learnt of Ralph's testimony against him, Ralph's own life would be in peril.

'I'm shutting the saloon,' Ralph announced now.

Collins shrugged. 'I don't—'

'I'm on that posse,' offered Hartford. 'That way I won't need to fret on what's happening. I'll know.'

Ralph shaped to walk to but his wife hurried into the saloon. Reaching Hartford, she grabbed a fistful of his shirt.

'I heard it all,' she screamed. 'No way are you going, mister!'

'I've got to, Amy,' Ralph snapped, trying to loosen her grip. 'I need to help find Auger.'

She slammed fists to his face then.

'No,' she howled. 'We've planned to get out of this hell town and I won't risk anything.' She stopped her assault, but her eyes sparked with rage. 'Let others risk their carcasses on account of that halfwit. You stay safe no matter what!'

Collins's countenance clouded. 'Ralph is loyal to Driftwood,' he said testily. 'Hell, he's raised in this town. I'd say—'

'Get to hell,' she screamed. She jabbed a hand. 'This town and all the dogs in it can go rot. All that matters is me and Ralph staying safe and getting our tearoom in Boston.'

Ralph angrily shoved his wife aside. He looked imploringly at the mayor then. 'That's not my thinking, Tom. You wouldn't—'

'It's OK.' Collins got to the batwings but then looked glumly back. 'You volunteered,' he grunted, 'and that counts.'

When he exited the saloon, Hartford and Amy bellowed abuse at each other. On the boardwalk, Collins watched as the posse men led their horses down Main Street. His guts turned with disquiet. Hell, he'd hired Sullivan to quell trouble but since the new sheriff hit town there'd been more killing and trouble in Driftwood than they'd seen for years. He set home then, musing nervously on what was still to come.

*

In the Circle C chuck hut, whiskey flowed. Meredith watched, dismayed, as Wade Lever and the ranch-hands drank to victory. Lever, getting steadily drunk, had words that slurred.

'I swore to get rid of Fraser. Hell, I shredded that bastard's back. Goddamn it, boys, did you hear the son of bitch beg?'

Meredith shook his head. He'd heard Fraser's pitiful screams, that man sent to a depravity of pain that many couldn't have endured. He'd survived, though, helped off the brand by Hall, and where a hurt man lives on his rage against those that made him suffer lingers too. Meredith had served the Circle C nigh on fifty years – worked for Seth Lomas's pa before Seth took over the brand. Meredith had witnessed it all in his tenure on the brand; he'd met all types of men. Fraser – singularly unstable – wasn't uncommon. Nor were the likes of Wade Lever.

Too certain by half, the brand foreman lacked the objectivity that made men proficient supervisors of others. With people like Lever, either your face fitted or it didn't. In Meredith's humble view, Lever would one day rile the wrong person and bring disaster upon them all. Over the years, simmering tensions between brand men often exploded into unmanageable violence where many died. It was that storm of vengeance that so blighted the untamed West. It was what they knew as a thunder of guns!

Stepping into the yard, Meredith headed for one of the small barns. He locked the door, sidled up the hayloft ladder and settled onto his bedroll. Let them drink, he mulled. Come dawn, Meredith C Lilley would be ready to do his duty.

As Meredith dropped off to sleep, Lever proposed a toast.

'To a pair of sons of bitches we kicked the hides off,' he called out, raising his shot glass. The others responded in kind. As their shot glasses clinked, a trio of horses walked down the stone-flecked road leading to the quadrangle.

'Now,' hissed Fraser with real steel to that word. 'We'll see how the other side screams!'

Her agitation growing, TJ sought her chance. It came when Sam broke the news to Aaron's pa. Auger Senior, collapsing with sobs into Sam Griffin's arms, was soon weeping in a seat.

'Oh, God,' he spluttered. 'He's out dawn to midnight most days. I ain't got any lariat of the boy but if anything should happen to Aaron I don't know what I'd do!'

'A posse's raised to bring the lad home,' reassured Sam. He glanced sharply at TJ then. 'Gal, get some coffee brewed.'

TJ nodded and set into the kitchen. She closed the door, tested the window and it slid open to a tug. Clambering out to the alley then, she ran as her feet touched dirt. At Main Street, she saw the road deserted but for two men standing guard. She ran towards the livery, ducking into another alley that would bring her to the back of the horse barn.

There, loosing a wall plank, she scuttled inside. With a lamp lit against the now settled dark of night, she saddled a horse. She moved to a hay bale – the one under which her pa stashed a Colt .41 with bullets. That tucked in her coat, she lifted the barn door's beam and led the horse out to the street.

'Hell, TJ,' one of the guards offered as she showed, 'where'd you think you're set to?'

'To help find Auger,' she grunted. The town's silence disquieted her and she said edgily, 'What the hell's happened?'

'Driftwood emptied when news of the killing got about; we're posted as a guard but it just ain't needed.' He fixed TJ with a questioning look. 'Take my advice, gal, those night plains ain't a place for a lady alone. Why don't you—' He left the rest unsaid as TJ vaulted into the saddle and drove her horse with heels and shouts. When she thundered the animal into the darkness beyond Main Street, the guard shrugged. 'Goddamn it, she wants to risk her neck, that's her stinking affair.'

TJ thought the same. She galloped her mount across the dark miles, knowing she'd help find Auger and keep Jeb safe. She'd achieve both this night, no matter what it took!

CHAPTER SEVENTEEN

Billy stilled his horse by the gallows gate and threw Fraser a scathing glare. Soon, Auger halting his own mount, they watched as Fraser jabbed out with his Colt.

'Why'd you boys stop?'

'This is madness,' hissed Billy. 'You've took our guns. What good are we if trouble starts?'

Fraser chuckled. 'As a shield against bullets you'll do well enough.' He clicked back his Colt's hammer and snarled, 'Move slow. Try anything and I'll spread your brains.'

Cursing, Billy urged his horse on at an amble. Auger quickly followed and before long, they came to a standstill in the yard. They waited then, hearing the raucous laughing drifting out of the chuck hut's open door.

Lever's hate-edged words sounded then: 'If that bastard Fraser or Hall ever show about here again, I'll beat them so bad they won't recognize each other!'

'But, Wade,' yelled another, 'I thought Lomas told you to lay off that pair till he got back. Won't the boss be raging you saw off those hawkers?'

'Hell, no,' spat back Lever. 'I did Lomas a favour. He'll get to see that.' He guffawed then and opined, 'Fraser was on his knees and crying like a baby. He won't—'

Fraser, the grind of his clenched teeth audible, moved fast. Off his horse, he gripped the Colt tightly as he sprinted the distance to the chuck hut door. Bursting through, he levelled the gun and growled, 'I ain't on my knees now. Soon it'll be you doing the crying.'

Lever, his drinking stilled, set the shot glass onto the tabletop. Soon, all of them wide-eyed with worry, the six ranch-hands quickly followed suit. One started to inch a hand to the gun strapped at his right hip then but Fraser, waggling the Colt, persuaded him otherwise.

'Hell, Fraser,' that same man muttered edgily now, 'It got out of hand. Wade never meant—'

'Goddamn I did.' Lever got to his feet and jabbed out a hand. 'You screamed, scum. I beat you bad and loved doing it.'

Fraser, eyes narrowing and only the slightest twitch at his jaw, growled, 'Yeah, I reckon you did.' He spat now before grunting, 'Now enjoy this!'

The Colt bucked in his grip, a bullet exiting the muzzle to a demonic roar. When the sent slug struck, scything into one of the ranch-hands, it sent the man crashing off a chair. He lay groaning on the boards then, seeping blood until he quickly died.

Lever battled back. Drawing fast, he levelled his .45 and slammed a finger to the trigger. As the gun roared, a slug hurtled out through a spew of flame and ripped the air mere inches from Fraser's head.

'Goddamn,' Lever bellowed as his shot missed. The

sent slug hammered into the hut's front wall at the same instant the ranch-hands lunged for their guns. Two hauled up their pistols in tandem, their blasted-out bullets hammering into the doorframe as Fraser spun on his heel and plunged out into the night's black yard.

He ran for his life. Reaching his skittered horse, he vaulted into the saddle then seethed with both elation and rage. One of his torturers was dead and in time, the others would die too. But while he'd begun to exact his bloody vengeance, Billy and Auger had fled.

Out of sight, they might be, but he could hear the clatter of hoofs on the stone-flecked approach road. He rode fast in pursuit now, driving his mount through the yard's gallows gate.

He turned in the saddle as he went, blasting as one of the ranch-hands plunged into the yard. Fraser's sent slug scythed home, biting into the ranch-hand's throat and sending him onto his knees. The hit man died spitting blood and cries, hands clutching his neck before he crashed face down on the yard's flaked-dry dirt.

'Bastards,' Fraser raged as his mount clattered to the top of the road. So many would perish before this night ended – those who'd scourged him for sure. Hall and Auger would die too.

'I'll find you, Billy boy,' he hissed as his horse reached grass and began to thunder across the miles. 'And when I do, you'll rue the day you ran out on Jake Fraser!'

He left a yard in turmoil. As a pall of gunsmoke thinned in the night's slight wind, Wade Lever hung his head. He proffered an unspoken prayer for his two dead men then, his eyes blazing.

121

'He's killed Tony and Garth,' he growled moments later. He looked up then, barking, 'We're hunting the son of a bitch down and I intend to settle this for good.'

Quickly, getting horses out of stalls and ready, they all got into the saddle. When they thundered out to the approach road, Meredith Lilley descended the loft ladder and walked outside. He moved silently between the chuck hut and the yard, frowning and eyeing the two corpses, his guts turning.

'I knew it,' he whispered, shaking his head. 'It's a goddamn thunder of guns!'

Sam left Auger Senior and returned to the livery at a jog trot. He opened up the barn, a quick check confirming his fears.

Goddamn, TJ, he cursed as he saw the empty stall in the horse barn. The love-crazed girl had set after the posse. He thought about saddling up himself and looking for her but quelled that idea quickly. Too old and his eyesight failing, he'd little chance. He'd just have to wait – like Auger Senior did – in the hope his offspring survived this night of madness. Later, seated on a hay bale he gripped a whiskey bottle with a trembling hand.

'Stay safe, gal,' he muttered as he let the bottle fall. 'I'll just die if anything happens to you!'

Jeb halted the posse with a bellowed shout. In time, horses stilled and snorted breath-clouds on those cold-gripped plains. They all waited, tense in the saddle. They'd made fast miles from Driftwood, positioned now a few hundred yards off the Circle C's eastern border.

A sound carried to them all now across that night-cloaked distance. It was the drumming of hoofbeats.

'Riders nearing,' one of the posse yelled, dragging up his rifle, 'I'll blast the sons of—'

'No,' Jeb bellowed. 'No shooting until we know who it is.'

Soon, all of them armed and with their guns readied, they waited, eleven citizens of Driftwood good and true, each with a finger twitching at his trigger.

They slowed their horses to a canter now. They'd ridden a withering pace, both animals struggling. They needed to let their mounts recover, Billy decided, worrying that another night's hard riding for his mare might kill the beast. They eased both horses to the walk, moved on a while until Billy stilled his mount. Auger soon did the same. They both listened intently then. A curse drifted to them in the wind, then the clink of horse gear.

'Jeez,' Billy's gasped curse was barely audible. 'Who is it?'

Aaron, trembling, his face dressed with sweat despite the cold, lowered a hand to his saddle-bag now. He fumbled a moment before lifting out a knife. He'd forgotten he'd had that. He proffered nothing to Billy, just gripped the knife by its Sheffield steel blade and waited.

A horse snorted in the dark ahead of them now, and Auger thought he defined a shape in the dark. A man in the saddle waited to blast Aaron to death. Auger's guts turned, and, flooded with panic, he swung back his arms and sent that knife whistling through the chilled night air.

'Oh, God!' a voice howled as the blade struck. 'I'm hit!'

Auger hauled reins then and rode, hurtling south. Billy cursed then rapidly followed.

Someone else sat on his stilled mount listening right then. Fraser, bristling with rage still, struggled to decipher the noises to his front. He listened, his gun to hand. Suddenly a critter screeched in the dark before a voice barked.

'Lassiter's stabbed. He's got a blade in his shoulder but he'll live.'

'They've set south,' another roared. 'We're setting after them, Sheriff Sullivan?'

Fraser straightened his gun arm and levelled his .45 into the dark. Sullivan was close, but clearly he had a host of others at his side. Fraser lowered the gun and slid it to its holster. When he took a shot at Sullivan, he wanted to be certain he killed that man. Fraser held and kept listening.

'A couple of you set back with Lassiter to Driftwood,' a voice ordered now. 'The rest of us will set south after those two, whoever they are.'

'It'll be Fraser and Hall,' another proffered. 'They'll swing for murder when we get them!'

Hoofbeats drummed on dry land now, soon fading to quiet. Fraser spat then at the underfoot of night-blackened grass.

He cursed to the news. Sullivan, a drifter made sheriff, rode the plains with a posse behind him. Fraser's eyes blazed. How'd Sullivan work out the truth? Maybe the lawman didn't; perhaps it was just a hunch. It didn't matter either way. Sullivan and the posse turned to the south, opening Driftwood to Jake's ambitions.

He waited then, watching shadowy forms fumbling just ahead.

'Come on,' one voice decried at length, 'we'll ride slow

and steady back to Driftwood.'

'Well, boys,' Fraser intoned softly as he began to follow, 'I'm right behind you every step of the way!'

CHAPTER EIGHTEEN

TJ wouldn't slacken the pace. With the ageing roan flagging to her cries and heels, she just kept driving it on. The beast tried, but the miles it'd already covered from Driftwood had taken their toll. Right then, on those night-swathed plains, the beast slumped, dropping hard to earth and spilling TJ out of the saddle. She crashed to the ground and lay there dazed and in pain. When she did finally sit up, she glanced nervously about and sighed with relief to see the roan upright and snorting nearby. It'd been a close call and she felt a stab of guilt to have worked the old horse as she had. Luckily, with steady riding, it would make the journey back to town.

She got to her feet with a groan, cursing her passion-driven stupidity. She'd charged out of Driftwood with little thought as to the risks or the anguish she'd cause to her pa. Jeb, she reasoned walking across to the horse, was a seasoned lawman. Hunting killers and hoodlums was his job. Her task was to wait with her pa for Jeb's return. He would return, she mused with certainty as she got back in the saddle. He'd vanquish any threat he faced.

She shaped to get the roan into a steady pace when

sounds pounded out of the dark surround. Voices drifted to her on the breeze and she dragged the rifle out of the saddle sheath and got the gun levelled. With her finger tracing the trigger, she quickly eased as the familiar tone of Edward Lassiter sounded out.

'Goddamn it,' the Driftwood resident groaned, 'a knife in me and I didn't see who threw it.' He proffered a curse then before grunting, 'I'm bleeding to death here.'

'Don't you worry, Ted,' a Driftwood man called Alf Graham reassured. 'Doc Jones will tend you in Driftwood.'

TJ, sliding the rifle back to the saddle, yelled out now, 'Mr Lassiter, Mr Graham – it's me, TJ.'

They loomed into view now, a trio of the posse with their mounts ambling.

'Land's sake, gal,' Alf Graham growled. 'What're you doing?' He and the other stilled their horses and Graham added, 'Sullivan and the rest of the posse are riding south. They're chasing Fraser and Hall.'

'What of Auger?' pressed TJ, her words layered with worry. 'Did you see him?'

Alf Graham shook his head. 'I guess Sullivan will keep looking once he's dealt with those two Circle C killers.' He nodded, certain then. 'Gal, you'd best set back into town with us.'

TJ nodded, began to drag the roan about when hoofs drummed a fast approach. Before TJ or the posse trio could get hands to guns, Jake Fraser showed, his Colt levelled.

'Howdy, people!'

'What in hell?' Alf Graham gasped. 'We thought you'd—'

'Wrong,' Fraser snarled. He jabbed his Colt at TJ now

and said, 'Now, why'd you be on these big, bad plains in the night?'

TJ's renowned feistiness overrode all her fears.

'Hunting scum like you,' she barked, 'to help—' She stopped short, but too late. Fraser guessed what she'd planned to say.

'To help Sullivan,' he drawled. 'Ain't that just grand – Sullivan having a little missy watching his back?' He urged his mount closer and said with a wink, 'I saw you visiting that sheriff's shack last night.' He chuckled now and grated, 'You a-loving of Sullivan; talk to me, missy . . . you a-loving than man?'

Alf Graham proffered a panicked gasp but TJ wouldn't be silenced now.

'Yes,' she snapped. 'I aim to marry him.'

Fraser sighed. 'Now, ain't that a damn. . . . You, a gal what dresses as a man set to wed that big ole lawman who's out there seeking to lay me in a grave.'

'He will, too,' raged TJ. Her eyes flashed anger in the dark and she spat, 'I told Jeb I reckoned you killed James Scott. I'm sure of it and that's why the posse's set to bring you in!'

Fraser proffered another sigh. 'Hell,' he muttered, 'it don't rightly matter that I tell you. I sure did knife that long-beard.' He tapped the front of his duster. 'Three thousand dollars is a damn good payday for anyone.' He nodded then. 'Mind, the six thousand your lover boy's going to pay will be better still.' He thumbed back his gun's hammer. 'Now, little missy, toss six-gun and rifle.'

Bristling, her fear rising as bile, TJ complied. Fraser turned the gun on the three posse men who did likewise. All of them unarmed now, Fraser nodded, satisfied.

'You'll need to get that stabbed man back to town!'

'Yeah,' growled Alf Graham edgily, 'The doc's got to stop the bleeding.'

'These physicians are useful,' Fraser intoned, 'if the need comes.' He shrugged, his eyes narrowing as he snarled, 'Mind, there're some spots a doc can't help you!'

'Dear God,' Alf Graham grunted, 'We don't—'

'Take hell,' Fraser cut in loudly. 'A doc ain't much good to you there!' He slammed a finger at the Colt's trigger and a slug exited through sheet flame and smoke. An instant later, the bullet slammed into Alf Graham's chest and sent him reeling back off his horse. He slammed to ground, howling and clutching at the wound. Lassiter perished then, a bullet decimating his head. The third Driftwood man bolted, dragging reins and driving his horse into the distance. He didn't make it. Fraser's gun barked again and a slug ripped into the fleeing man's spine. Soon, gunsmoke and cordite thinning in the breeze, Fraser jabbed the Colt at TJ.

'We're set to Driftwood,' he snarled. 'I aim to get my money.'

TJ's tears started as they rode. She thought despairingly on the three good Driftwood citizens slaughtered on that plain. She thought of poor haunted Aaron Auger probably hiding in the night for fear of his own life. She thought of Jeb and she ached for him. But he had to stay away. Fraser was clearly capable of any bloody outrage and whilst Jeb stayed out of town, he'd be safe.

'Kill me if that's your aim,' she mumbled as they closed on the edge of town. 'I'll die gladly if it'll keep Jeb safe.'

Fraser snorted. 'When I'm finished with you, little missy,' he growled, 'you'll be right glad to die right enough.'

TJ's guts turned and she willed this nightmare to end. She clamped her eyes shut, trying to drown the panic that swamped her.

They'd driven their mounts headlong to Driftwood but halted in the saddle now. That barrage of gun blasts had set them on edge and now they surveyed the trio of corpses.

'Hell's teeth,' growled Lever, easing out of the saddle to take a closer look. He prodded each body with a boot before intoning sourly, 'Alf Graham, Ted Lassiter and Bill Sweeney.'

The four surviving Circle C hands, sitting disquieted in the saddle, all cursed the carnage and willed this hellish night to end. When it did, they prayed they'd all still be living. They'd each enjoyed the pain and humiliation inflicted on that abrasive bastard Jake Fraser when it happened but the consequences of it were now starkly clear. Now, it seemed, the carnage Fraser had enacted at the Circle C he'd repeated here on the grass a couple of miles outside of Driftwood. And even if they all emerged unscathed from this firestorm of killing, they feared Seth Lomas's reaction when the brand boss rode back from Dodge.

'It ain't in doubt this is Fraser's doing,' growled Wade Lever, rejoining his horse. 'That man's goddamn crazed.'

'We shouldn't have whipped the son of a bitch,' one of the ranch-hands offered edgily. 'You set Fraser over the edge. Hell's sake, what's the boss going to say?'

Lever spat at the underfoot of parched grass and snarled, 'I told you – I'll sort Lomas. My aim is Fraser. We'll kill that dog and I reckon that man's in Driftwood right about now!'

'And this new law in town?' one of the hands grunted. Only that morning, a trader delivering a wagon of food stores to Meredith Lilley spoke of Jeb Sullivan. 'This sheriff looks useful with a gun. It's said he blasted three men already. I'd reckon to report those killings and let him hunt Fraser and Hall.'

Wade Lever's eyes sparked with fury. 'You do as I say,' he barked whilst jabbing a hand. 'I don't need an in-comer, even if he's got a stinking badge pinned on. Fraser killed our boys; for that, he dies. Now, you sons of bitches, we ride.'

They all battled their fears then and moved their horses forward. Lever's own guts churned but for a different reason. He felt hate and the want of revenge rise as bile. Fraser would be in hell this night, no matter what it took!

Resting their mounts close by a clump of cottonwood, Billy struggled to make some sense of it all. He'd caught up with Auger, only stopping the kid by grabbing a hand to his reins. They'd ridden on at a sane pace then, but even so their shattered horses needed time to recover. As Billy sought answers, next to him, with his head slumped, Aaron wept steadily.

'I didn't mean it,' Auger sobbed at length. 'It just happened. You don't think that I—'

'Hell knows,' Billy cut in, annoyed. 'You chuck a knife in the goddamn dark, what did you expect?' He quelled his ire then and grunted, 'Maybe you just winged that man.'

Auger stemmed his tears. 'Who the hell were they?'

'They rode a line out of Driftwood,' Billy reasoned now.

131

'I'd say it was posse!'

Auger's hopes soared. 'We'll tell them the truth. You'll swear Fraser slew James Scott and it'll be OK, won't it?'

'Maybe,' drawled Billy. 'The thing is, out here in the night I don't aim to take any chances.' He jabbed a hand. 'Fraser is somewhere near and he'll kill us both at a spit; Wade Lever and the Circle C boys too. You've sent a knife into one of the posse so they'll be in no mood to listen. They'll blast first and ask questions later.'

'What do we do then?' Auger cried. 'I don't want to die!'

'Listen,' said Billy solemnly then. 'If that posse man's OK then it stands that neither of us killed a soul and we've got to make this new sheriff see that.' He shook his head then. 'It's a risk for sure but I'd say our best chance is in town!'

'In Driftwood?' Auger howled, 'how can you—'

'You keep riding if you want, kid,' Billy snapped. 'I'd fancy we'd get a better chance in Driftwood.' He dragged reins but halted as Auger cried out.

'There's a dried creek. It'll get us to town fast.'

Billy's tone was solemn. 'Before that posse catches up?'

Aaron shrugged as they rode. 'I sure hope so!'

CHAPTER NINETEEN

'Goddamn it, Amy, that's enough!'

She glowered, defiant. 'Let them get to hell,' she screamed. 'We're safe and that's all that matters!'

Hartford reddened with fury. Their argument raging in the corridor behind the long bar, he jabbed a hand.

'We're citizens of Driftwood,' he barked, 'and that means responsibilities. This town survives because the strong stand for the weak. You'd let Auger—'

'Yes,' she howled, slamming her fists to his face, 'they can all die. We live and that's all that matters.'

She stalked off and Hartford battled his rage. He moved agitatedly behind the counter and considered his empty saloon. He doused the lamps now, sure no custom would ensue this night.

'I won't go,' he said with certainty then. 'Let her scream till she's blue. I'll not desert Driftwood in its hour of need!'

Jeb halted the posse with a shout. Now, by a clump of cottonwood, he allowed their horses to rest and tried to fashion some sense out of it all.

'They've taken the dried river-bed,' yelled out a man. 'I'd reckon they're set into Driftwood!'

Jeb shook his head. 'But that don't—'

'I don't goddamn know,' the man bellowed a retort. 'Fraser's crazy, ain't he?' He jabbed out a hand. 'We'd best get back to town fast. There ain't no telling what the man's capable of.'

'What about Auger?' another offered uneasily. 'We'll give up the search?'

'Fraser and Hall first,' said Jeb decisively. 'Once that pair are under lock and key we'll resume the search for Aaron.'

All jerking reins, they descended into the river course and rode towards Driftwood. Each man prayed as they crossed the distance, just willing they'd be in time!

On Driftwood's deserted Main Street, Fraser stilled both their horses. He shook his head then. 'It's hellish quiet.'

'All account of you,' snapped TJ with defiance. 'Jeb cleared the town of some scum. You killing Scott did for the rest!'

'That's not good for trade,' chuckled Fraser, 'but useful for me.' He jabbed a hand at the saloon then. 'A couple of whiskies and I'll—' His words choked off, and he watched, on edge, as the two-man guard stepped out of the board-walk shadows.

TJ gasped, her gaze set to the livery then. Light flooded out through the flung-open doors of the horse barn and TJ willed her pa to slam them shut and set down the locking beam. She prayed he'd stay safe.

'Gal,' one of the guards bellowed as they drew nearer, both with their rifles to hand. 'Is that you back?'

'Yeah,' she said tremulously. 'It didn't work out.'

The two town guards halted, one grunting, 'Who's aside you?' A moment later, when no answer came, the click of their guns broke the quiet.

Fraser moved quickly then. He grabbed a fistful of TJ's hair, hurtling off his horse and dragging her, screaming, with him. When they both hit the dirt of Main Street, Fraser dragged up his gun, set the muzzle end to her head and snarled, 'Now, boys, you'll stay steady there lessen you want this little missy dead.'

'Goddamn Fraser,' spat one guard. He levelled his Carbine but stayed from firing.

'No,' his partner gasped. 'We'll not put TJ at risk.'

'Good,' growled Fraser. 'I'm set into the saloon with this girl. You two hold there with your guns ready!'

'Hold – what in goddamn for?'

Fraser sighed. 'My partner Billy Hall is riding hell for leather this way with a heck of men aside him.' Fraser added with a grunt, 'They ain't in the mood for talking.'

'What the hell's going on?' barked one of the guards. 'What do you and Hall want?'

'I want the bank manager at the saloon first,' barked Fraser. 'When that's done, I want Hall and those cutthroats he rides with stopped before they spill blood in this town!'

'Spill blood? Hell's sake, why'd he want to—'

'He's crazy,' Fraser bellowed now. 'Listen, goddamn it, you ain't going to have the time to ask questions. Lessen you bring Hall down there'll be carnage in Driftwood this night.' He moved to the street's edge, dragging TJ up the steps to the boardwalk. At the batwings of the saloon, he cursed as one of the guards sprinted off into the shadows.

The other stayed where he was.

'Lee's set to get the bank manager,' the now lone guard yelled, 'you just swear not to harm TJ.'

'I won't,' retorted Fraser pushing into the saloon and hauling the grunting TJ with him.

The guard shook his head and he half-turned. He halted through, gazing morosely back at the batwings as Fraser's foreboding words drifted out of the saloon.

'I won't hurt this little missy. But Billy Hall and those men he rides with will kill her. There ain't a goddamn thing I can do about that!'

Sam, seated on a hay bale in the horse barn, had agonized for what seemed like an age. Earlier, out on Main Street, he'd met and questioned the two guards Sullivan deployed. They'd confirmed the worst: TJ had ridden out of town with a vow to find the posse.

Sam had returned to the livery with that shocking news and tried in vain to occupy himself with work. He ached for his daughter, though, and every moment he battled the urge to get on a horse and ride out to the plains to hunt for her. But he dismissed this as futile. A needle in a haystack sprang to mind and he struggled against the well of tears in his eyes. He cursed his headstrong daughter and his own failure to keep her in check. He cursed Sullivan, too, for turning TJ's head and causing her to place herself at such risk.

Spitting now at the floor, Sam railed against his own stupid reasoning. That TJ had fallen head over heels for Sullivan was the way it was! Sullivan was the only hope Driftwood had to break the shackles of downward decline and the hoodlums and thugs that blighted its streets. God willing, somehow, out of this nightmare time TJ would emerge unscathed and she and Sullivan would wed in a town tamed.

He moved towards the livery doors, musing on those shouts in Main Street he'd just overheard. Peering out, he stared down the partially illuminated thoroughfare and saw one of the guards maintaining a still vigil in the centre of the road.

'Hey,' Sam yelled now. 'What's going on?'

The guard turned and shook his head. 'Go inside and try and keep yourself busy, Mr Griffin.'

'Goddamn it,' barked Sam, 'could you settle to anything with your only child out there on them plains!'

The guard shaped his lips to reply when Collins and the other guard rushed from a side street. Collins halted, saw Sam and walked across to him.

'Lee tried to get Albert Lloyd to come but he wouldn't, Sam. I'll do something about that, I swear.' Sam's perplexed look made the mayor add, 'We'll get TJ safe, Sam.'

Griffin nodded. 'You'll raise more men to look for her?'

'Look for her – hell, she's in the saloon, Sam.'

The ageing liveryman, the world seeming to lurch, almost fell. Rapidly then, with his composure regained, Sam blustered, 'I didn't—' He lurched towards the Regency Palace Saloon, but Collins and the guard restrained him.

'Don't be a fool,' barked Collins. 'You rush the saloon he'll kill her straight out.'

'Kill,' howled Sam. 'Who in hell?'

'Fraser,' intoned Collins sombrely. 'He's got TJ hostage. Now, you want to do something, get your rifle.'

Sam did. Soon, he, Collins and the two guards held a

line on Main Street and all of them bearing arms. Now they waited.

'Hall's intending to slaughter all he can,' the mayor pressed softly after a few moments. 'That's what Fraser said?'

'Yeah,' one of the guards grunted sourly. 'He said there'd be blood spilt in Driftwood.'

'We haven't got a choice, then,' returned Collins, gripping his gun tightly. 'I reckon we all know what we need to do!'

None answered. They knew exactly what that meant.

CHAPTER TWENTY

Off-saddling at the edge of town, Auger led the way. Leading their mounts by the reins, Aaron navigated Driftwood's jet-black alleys until they'd reached the small barn standing at the back of the shack he shared with his pa. With the horses tended, fed and in stalls, Billy followed Aaron to the shack's front door. Soon, both stepping inside, Billy saw an old man, his face etched with hurt, slumped in a rocking chair.

As their footsteps thumped on the boards, the old man looked around and a spark of salvation showed in his eyes.

'Oh God,' old man Auger spluttered, struggling to stand, 'I just can't—'

Aaron, throwing himself forward, sank to his knees and gripped his pa into a lingering hug.

'I'm safe,' Aaron sobbed. 'It's OK now.'

They eased apart and Mr Auger shook his head. 'How'd you get back, boy? Dear Lord, what's been happening?'

'I can't explain it all, Pa,' Aaron returned with a nod. 'As for my getting safe it's down to Mr Hall here.'

Billy, standing by the door proffered a shrug. 'Say,' he

muttered now, 'Mr Auger, would you have a gun I could use?'

'The sideboard over there,' said Auger Senior, jabbing a bony hand. 'Top drawer – it's a Remington with a few bullets.'

Soon, that weapon to hand, Billy got back to the shack door. 'Don't let this boy out your sight, Mr Auger.'

'I won't.'

Aaron nodded and watched as Billy plunged into the night, the shack door slamming shut behind him.

'Stay alive, Billy,' he whispered, 'you're the proof I need!'

Hartford, fear churning his guts, watched as Fraser slapped off TJ's wide-brim and tried to smother her face with kisses. She battled back, clawing nails to his face. He reacted angrily – slamming a fist to her face and dropping her to her knees. She spat blood, groaned and her head slumped.

'Hey, 'keep,' Fraser snarled now, 'get whiskey poured.'

Soon, dragging TJ into a chair, Fraser waited. With the drink delivered, he quaffed it fast and gasped as the fluid burned in his guts. He waggled the gun at Hartford.

'Just you in here?' he growled.

'My wife,' Hartford said edgily, 'she's—' He stopped short and blustered, 'But she ain't—'

Fraser's eyes narrowed. 'Get the bitch in here. And don't reckon to garner a gun.' He set the Colt's muzzle to TJ's blood-dressed face. 'Any trouble and I'll blow missy's head off!'

Hartford, grim-faced, proffered a nod. He moved away then, exiting the bar and ascending steps to their living quarters on the Regency Palace's second floor. In one room, he dragged Amy up from a sofa.

'What're you doing?' she barked.

'You're needed downstairs,' he said testily. 'Hurry, woman.'

He hauled her along a corridor and down the stairs to the rear of the long bar. She defied him there, punching and clawing until he released his hold.

'What's going on?' she snapped. 'I won't take another step lessen you tell me!'

So he did. When he drawled off, she shook her head violently and jabbed a hand at a door that led out to an alleyway.

'We'll sneak off,' she hissed. 'We'll get safe and leave that livery bitch to it!'

Ralph's face flashed with rage. He shoved past her and barked, 'You run if you want, Amy. TJ needs me and I won't leave her now.' His eyes sparked with determination. 'I'll not abandon Driftwood either.' He shaped to enter the bar but Amy launched herself at him, hammering him with blows.

'You stupid hick bastard,' she screamed. 'We get a chance to escape and save our hides and you turn your nose to it. Let these stinking Driftwood scum go to hell. Not me!' She plunged out through the door and disappeared into the dark alley.

Hartford shaped lips to bellow her back but realized it wouldn't change anything. He shut the door and then walked sombrely back into the saloon. He eyed Fraser pleadingly before saying softly, 'My wife's—'

He didn't get to finish. A noise made Fraser rush to the batwings and the outlaw gazed out, intrigued. When he looked back, his eyes sparked.

'It's going to start,' he said with a voice edged with levity. 'Any goddamn second now!'

They halted their horses in line about five hundred yards off Driftwood's western edge.

'Right,' growled Wade Lever. 'Fraser and Hall die. We ride in at a gallop and blasting guns. We'll storm this town.'

The four ranch-hands bristled with unease. They all mulled despondently on the same thing – rage commanded Lever's actions now. For his want of revenge, they could all die this night. Each mused sombrely. Lever, with total control of the brand and men in Lomas's absence, held complete sway. If they refused to obey his orders, they'd be dismissed without pay.

When Lever bellowed the order, the four ranch-hands got pistols to hand and nervously thumbed back the hammers.

'Now!' the foreman roared, driving his mount fast along Main Street. 'Ride on, boys!'

They charged, reins in one hand and guns in the other. When they thundered forward in a maelstrom of dust, each levelled their weapons and slammed fingers to the triggers. A second later, Driftwood's thoroughfare exploded to flame spurts and noise. Hell had come to town!

And hell came back with a vengeance.

'Fire!' Collins howled above the cacophonous clatter of muzzle blasts.

With screaming bullets shredding through the night's chilled air, people started to die. One of the ranch-hands howled, crashing off his horse as a slug thundered into his guts. He perished where he fell, a brief twitch of his body as the life jerked out of him.

Collins, who'd not shot his gun for a heck of years, dispatched a slug that bit flesh out of a Circle C man's arm but he stayed in the saddle. Bellowing with pain, the struck rider managed to drag reins and drive his mount with headlong speed back out of town.

When Sam loosed his rifle, he staggered backward with the recoil but grinned, content as a pained cry sounded. An instant later, Wade Lever struck in the neck, he slumped off his horse and hit the dirt with a sickening thud. He died vomiting blood, his body writhing to the last.

The other two Circle C men fled. They turned their horses with screams and curses, soon exiting Driftwood to escape to the plains.

When all quieted, Main Street's air thick with cordite and smoke, Collins stepped forward. The others followed and before long they all gazed down, appalled at the corpses of Wade Lever and the slain Circle C man, Clem Lewis.

'Damn it,' spat Collins, anguish evident in those words. 'It's Lever and Lewis. How the hell could we know?' He looked imploringly at Sam and the two town guards. 'They rode into town blasting guns. We'd gotten no choice!'

One of the guards, dropping his rifle, held his head in his hands. 'God alive – Fraser set this up. He pledged Billy Hall came to spread blood in Driftwood and I'd reckon that—'

'It was all lies!' Fraser shouted, crashing out through the batwings, dragging TJ with him. On the boardwalk he laughed. 'You blasted brand men.' He jabbed his free hand at Lever's corpse. 'I meant to kill that bastard myself but I'm happy enough.'

'You'll swing,' snarled one of the guards now. 'We've killed innocent men on account of you!'

'Innocent?' grunted Fraser with a shrug. 'Hell, I'd say Lever's in hell right enough.' He retreated now, only pausing to shift his grip from TJ's coat to her hair. He hauled her, screaming, in through the saloon's swing doors.

'God,' howled Collins, 'what'll it take for you to let TJ go?'

'If I don't see your bank manager,' Fraser's voice barked its reply, 'this little missy dies.'

Collins grimaced. He studied the dead again and his guts turned. He lurched away then, setting towards a side street, knowing that Albert Lloyd, who'd refused already to assist, would need some persuading to open up the bank. He just had to, though. If Lloyd refused, TJ Griffin would die this night.

That firestorm of gun blasts stunned them all. Right then, the posse now out of the saddle and their mounts lashed at the back of town, they all halted in an alley and battled panic about the fate of their own families.

'Jeez,' one middle-ager spat, 'that shooting's in Main Street. It's got to be Fraser and Hall.' He began to move off, his rifle to hand. 'I'm set to protect my wife and child; I'll not risk my kin with those killers in Driftwood.'

More posse men deserted now. As they hurried away, just Jeb and one other remained. Garth Kennedy, a twenty-two-year-old who worked the counter at Collins's hardware, proffered a shrug.

'I ain't got family,' he said. 'It's down to us two, Sheriff.'

Grim-faced, Jeb returned a nod. He ached to run himself, to get to the livery and check that TJ was safe. First, though, he'd have to face the aftermath of that barrage of shooting. He imagined widespread killings, Fraser and Hall butchering all they met.

'OK,' he grunted to Kennedy now, 'we'll set to Main Street. Only then will we know what we're facing.'

When they walked, both with guns to hand, they both bristled with tension. What lay ahead they couldn't know. They'd face it head-on, though; they'd bring Fraser and Hall to justice or die trying!

Hartford was now seated beside TJ at one of the saloon's tables, Fraser slouched at the bar, re-topping his glass from a whiskey bottle he'd lifted from a shelf.

'It's all messed up,' he slurred as the whiskey began to bite. 'My best plans blown open.' He set his shot glass on the counter then belched. 'I'll not go empty-handed, mind. I need a heck of dollars for where I'm going!'

'You won't need money in hell,' TJ mumbled, battling the pain in her face. She sniffed against the blood leaking from her nose before saying at the edge of tears, 'When my man gets here you'll be leaving the world for good!'

Fraser proffered a laugh. 'You're full of it ain't you, livery bitch!' He glanced about then and jabbed his gun at Hartford. 'Talking of bitches. . . .'

'Amy,' Hartford gasped, his face muscles twitching. 'She just ran for it, Mr Fraser. 'There weren't a thing I could do!'

Fraser's eyes widened but he stilled his ire. Shrugging

then he growled, 'So be it. I've gotten you two as hostage and when that bank man gets here we'll get this finished with.' He rambled on then, his words getting slower as the liquor took over. He spoke about his Mexican dream – how he'd retire there to live like a king. 'That's the way of it,' he ended with a snarl. 'I ain't working my fingers to the bone for a few bits. I'll have what I can get and I'll do what it takes to get it!'

'You hurt and kill decent people for your own gain,' spat TJ, fear and rage turning her guts. 'Driftwood was a good place till the likes of you set here. When Jeb gets this town turned about we'll be decent again.'

Fraser waggled the gun. 'What's that to me – I'll be in my kingdom, won't I?'

TJ, her head slumped now, ached for Jeb. She willed him to vacate those vast, night-clothed plains and to get to Driftwood. She wanted and needed him close – to both save her life and end Fraser's psychopathic existence.

My darling, she intoned without words, *I know you can hear me. Please, get here soon!*

She ran, cursing this dog-dirt town and her scum of a husband. She dropped to her knees in an alley as gun blasts deafened the night. When that noise subsided, she worked her way towards the periphery of town.

She cursed her life now. Why she'd wed the bastard Hartford she'd never really understood. She'd reckoned him wealthy – the chicken farm, then the saloon. But he lacked imagination. Ralph, a Midwest fool, was content to end his days on these plains that baked by day and often froze to hell by night.

'He and Driftwood can get to hell,' she cursed now as

she ran. She'd hide this night in someone's barn. Tomorrow, when whatever nightmare that beset Driftwood was long finished with, she'd withdraw her savings from the bank and get the next stage East. She'd settle with her sister until she found another man to marry. He'd be classy and possessed of real wealth!

She gasped as she struggled onward, moving through those narrow passageways at the edge of town.

'Stinking, no-good sons of hick bitches,' she snarled aloud as she left one alley and turned into another. 'Every stinking scum piece of dirt in this town can get to hell!' She shaped her lips to curse again when a flash of flame erupted from the black confines of that passage. She whined then and slumped to her knees, her hands exploring the bloody wound at her guts.

'Oh, God,' she gasped, her eyes dimming as she crashed face down onto the dirt. 'Why did this—' She choked off in death, spreading blood onto the dust.

Soon, Jeb sprinted forward whilst a panicked Kennedy tentatively followed.

'Oh, God,' Kennedy howled as he gazed down at Amy Hartford's felled form. 'I didn't know; I just didn't—'

'Damn it,' snapped Jeb, kneeling beside the body. 'Why the hell did you shoot?'

Even as he'd said it Jeb realized the futility of the question. With a decade of law experience behind him, he'd the gun skill and speed to stay his finger at the trigger until he'd assessed risk. For the ordinary citizenry like Garth Kennedy, that would never be so. When someone plunged towards them through the dark of the alley Kennedy's panic guided his actions. He'd drawn and fired before Jeb could stop him.

147

Kennedy, trembling, gasped, 'Please tell me she ain't—'

'Dead,' grunted Jeb standing again. 'Who was it?'

'It's Amy Hartford from the saloon.' Kennedy's body was racked with sobs. 'I don't know how I'll live with myself. I just don't—'

'Stay those tears,' barked Jeb testily now. 'I need you with your head steady from here on in.'

Kennedy nodded. 'OK, Sullivan, I'm with you.' He jabbed his gun at the dead woman now and said edgily, 'God, but she was easy to dislike. I wouldn't wish her dead, though!'

Jeb nodded grimly. 'We'll set back for the body after we've dealt with Fraser and Hall.' He jabbed a hand and said with venom then, 'All trouble ends in Driftwood this night!'

CHAPTER TWENTY-ONE

Billy, his gun to hand, held in the shadows at the edge of Main Street. He jumped as a gun blast echoed out of an alley, but as the noise quietened, he tried to drive all thoughts of it from his mind. Who'd shot and at whom he couldn't dwell on now.

He concentrated on the people in the thoroughfare now. Two men armed with rifles were there alongside the old man from the livery, he brandishing a Winchester.

Others bustled into view then – Mayor Collins with the manager of the bank beside him.

'I've brought Albert Lloyd,' Collins bellowed then, 'he'll open the bank and get money to make Fraser leave.'

'Damn it, no,' one of the guards exploded then with a curse. 'We can't let Fraser get away with this. We'll just let him take what he wants from the vaults and ride out of town?'

'But he's got TJ hostage and Ralph Hartford too,' howled Collins. 'That gun blast at the back of town. Any ideas what that's about?'

'No,' Sam Griffin grunted. 'Likely it's Fraser's partner

149

Billy Hall.'

Billy eased into view, his gun levelled but his voice calm. 'It weren't me,' he said boldly, stepping forward.

They all tensed as he neared.

'I don't mean to shoot,' said Billy with a nod, 'lessen you draw on me first. I just want to be heard out.'

'Go on,' grunted Mayor Collins. 'It's time for explaining, I reckon.'

'I rode with Fraser,' said Billy with a shrug. 'That's until tonight. I split to save Auger's life.'

'Aaron,' gasped Collins. 'He's OK?'

'At home with his pa,' drawled Billy. 'Fraser knifed that miner out on the plains and I guess that kid just came across the body. Hell, that boy's a windbag and that's about it!'

Collins nodded but he looked glum. 'Lever and those other Circle C men,' he said testily, 'why'd they set into town in rage and blasting their guns!'

'Fraser shot two brand men back at the ranch,' grunted Billy. 'Lever had Fraser whipped and for that men die!'

'And you,' pressed Collins, 'you've no blood on your hands?'

Billy shook his head. 'I only wanted to earn me a farm. I'd work hard, hell I would, to earn honest dollar!'

'What,' said Sam testily, 'are your intentions now?'

'To kill Fraser,' said Billy, his eyes sparking with determination, 'before he harms anyone else.'

The surviving Circle C men, shocked but determined, angled their mounts back to Driftwood. They off-saddled at a clump of trees just outside the town and, leaving their mounts, they stole forward on foot, rifles to hand.

Now, edging through the black to the point where the

grass and dust of Main Street joined, all knelt and levelled their guns.

'What now?' one of them hissed. 'Lever's dead for sure!'

'We've got to make sure,' another growled. 'We need to check on Tommy too.'

They edged forward with tentative steps. Near the saloon, sighting the crowd milling about, one ranch-hand bellowed, 'You killed Lever and Tom?'

The two guards answered with their rifles levelled and were soon blazing slugs through flame. The Circle C men responded in kind. One guard howled as a bullet thudded into his chest, and a second later he crashed to the street where he died with a strangled cry. The other guard crashed to ground as he bolted for cover, a bullet hammering into his spine.

Collins, helping Sam Griffin, ran for his life. He got to the livery, dragging Sam inside, and they shut the doors and slammed the locking beam into place.

Albert Lloyd froze. He stood, paralyzed by fear, in Main Street. That statuesque pose broke only when Billy sprinted forward and grabbed a handful of the bank manager's shirt. Lloyd cried and begged then as Billy dragged him up the boardwalk steps and into the saloon.

As they crashed the batwings, they both faced an armed and agitated Jake Fraser.

'What in God's holy name—' Fraser snarled, levelling his drawn six-gun at Billy. 'I didn't reckon to see you again less I caught you to kill!'

'I got this bastard,' Billy snarled, throwing Albert Lloyd to the boards. As Lloyd hit the timbers with a grunt, Billy delivered a boot to the back. With Lloyd bellowing in pain,

Billy said through gritted teeth, 'Mr Bank Manager, you'll open that bank and give me and Fraser what we want!'

Fraser's eyes widened and confusion darkened his face.

'Hell, Billy,' he grunted, 'I can't reckon this out.' He sighed, lowered his gun and said testily, 'I don't know what to reckon. I thought you'd ridden out on me, kid!'

'You stupid bastard,' Billy snarled, jabbing the Remington at Fraser then. 'You take my guns; you planned to slay me before we got to Mexico, too. Well, it ain't happening, Jake. I'll have my share of the dollars and then I'm set to Montana.'

Fraser's look was unreadable. A moment later, he said edgily, 'That halfwit kid, what did you do with him?'

Billy shrugged. 'He's critter food. I caught him and snapped his neck with my hands.' He moved fast then, hauling the bank man up and slamming him into a chair next to TJ.

TJ emitted a low howl whilst Lloyd incanted a softly uttered prayer. Billy, facing Hartford, who stood rigid behind the counter, spat with venom now, 'You too, fat man, get in a seat aside these two curs.'

Fraser's eyes flashed with a mix of doubt and confusion. A moment later he grunted, 'I'll be straight with you, Billy boy, I reckoned you a problem and when you rode out on me at the Circle C I'd planned your end right enough.'

'The halfwit got away when you started blasting,' snapped Billy. 'I went after to chase the son of a bitch down!'

'And now you're square aside me, Bill?'

Billy shrugged. 'I want dollars, Jake. When it's done we'll share out as equals and ride our own ways.'

Fraser nodded and inched toward the swing doors.

'Those gun blasts outside,' he growled, peering over the batwings. 'What the hell's going on?'

'Wade Lever's boys – they ain't in the mind to talk, I'd say!'

Fraser nodded, saw two blurred shapes move out of an alleyway onto Main Street.

He glanced sharply at Billy and said with a nod, 'I'd say the solution's just arrived!'

They stood shoulder to shoulder on that midnight road. Jeb perused the bodies littering the thoroughfare. They'd completed the last few feet at the sprint, that last cataclysm of gun blasts spurring both him and Kennedy on. Now, faced with four corpses, Jeb shook his head.

'I just don't—'

'The two locals you posted as a guard,' said Kennedy. He jabbed a hand further along the street. 'That's Wade Lever and one of the fellers off the Circle C.'

Jeb couldn't fashion any sense and he began to inch forward. He halted then, a yell stilling him. Sam showed through the partly opened doors of the livery barn.

'Fraser's got TJ hostage in the saloon,' cried Griffin.

Jeb sprinted then, making the distance to the livery and demanding answers.

With all explained, Mayor Collins said sourly, 'When Hall showed he professed he'd help kill Fraser. Then those Circle C men came blasting guns again. The two guard men are dead. As for Hall and Albert Lloyd I can't say!'

'Maybe they've hid in one of the alleys,' reasoned Jeb. 'Can you work your way to the Auger place to make sure that Aaron's safe? Hell, if he is that'll mean Hall's telling the truth.'

Mayor Collins nodded. 'Sam and me will get out the

back of the livery and get that done. You just be careful. Those Circle C men are still on Main Street and shooting at anything that moves.'

'My gal,' gasped Sam, grabbing Jeb's arm then, 'Goddamn it, Sullivan, don't you try to be no hero and put her at—'

'Get to Auger's place,' Jeb barked. As they scuttled out through the barn, Jeb ran onto the street. He halted then, watching in dismay as Garth Kennedy strode down the middle of Main Street with his gun levelled.

'Goddamn it,' Jeb howled. 'What are you doing?'

If Kennedy heard, he didn't have time to reply. Flames spewed out in the distance and Kennedy, dropping to his knees, groaned once before crashing face down and dead onto the dust.

Jeb sprinted into action then. He hurtled down Main Street, his Colt roaring out slugs. One of the Circle C men, howling demonically as a slug struck his head, died with his brains spilled. The other two ran for cover, one hiding behind a rain barrel whilst the other squatted at the entrance to an alley. Soon, left alone in the street, Jeb paced inexorably forward. His way strewn with corpses, he thought only of killing others.

'Lay down your guns,' he yelled, 'or so help me you'll die.'

They answered with more fire, a volley of shots whistling slugs down that street. Jeb, ducking fast and then settling on one knee, now fired with a decade's skill and training. Both Circle C men perished with bullets to their hearts. With the killing over, Jeb set his sights on the saloon.

'Now,' he growled, striding toward the batwings, 'it all ends!'

CHAPTER TWENTY-TWO

'It's a goddamn bloodbath out there,' grunted Billy. He'd replaced Fraser at the batwings, watching appalled at the killing outside. 'I reckon not a thing's stayed alive!'

Dropping with a grunt to a chair, Fraser appraised TJ, Hartford and Lloyd in turn. They all sat slumped in seats, TJ still weeping while Lloyd rocked and proffered a low, mournful moan. Hartford sat upright, his face paled and beaded with sweat. Fraser studied Billy then and gave a sigh. He couldn't decipher the change. Billy, for months demurring against violence and crime, now seemed to seek it more that Fraser himself. Fraser's eyes narrowed and he growled, 'I can't make it out, Billy boy.'

'What the hell d'you mean?' Billy, looking around from the batwings, possessed eyes blazing with rage. 'I killed Auger, didn't I? I set here with that bank man. What more d'you want?'

Fraser jabbed the gun at TJ. 'Beat this bitch!'

Billy faltered. 'But, Jake, I don't—'

'Beat her,' screamed Fraser. 'I need goddamn proof!'

Billy sighed, stepped across the saloon and grabbed a

155

fistful of TJ's duster. He slammed a fist to her head then, driving her off the chair. As she hit the boards, Billy followed up with a boot to her back.

'More,' chuckled Fraser.

A few more kicks satisfied the sadist and left TJ groaning and weeping on the floor.

'You bastard,' screamed Hartford, on his feet and with both fists clenched. 'No man should treat a woman—' His words strangled off as Fraser's gun slammed out a bullet. With Ralph dead beside the table, Fraser nodded.

'You bring the livery bitch; we set out together.'

Soon, out on the boardwalk of the body-strewn Main Street, they halted as they sighted the man with a badge on his coat.

'So you're Mr high and mighty Sullivan?' Fraser shrugged. 'As you can see, Sheriff, we got your bank manager and your bitch. We aim to get some dollars and then get the hell out of here.'

Jeb's rage quelled. His law experience took over now. TJ became another victim he needed to rescue. He glanced at TJ's bruised, bloodied and sagging form and dismissed the personal connection to her.

'Carnage,' Jeb said steadily then. 'All these people dead on account of a piece of scum like you.'

Fraser chuckled. 'The thing is, Sullivan, whatever critter-laden town a man sets to there're tinder-dry grudges you can put a match to. Afore you know it, the whole damn land's ablaze with hate and blood.'

'Including your own,' said Jeb with venom. 'You reckon I'll let you ride out of here?'

Fraser nodded at Billy and he landed a fist to her back, making her scream. 'With this little missy in our hold I'd reckon so.'

They moved along the boardwalk, reaching the bank whilst Jeb matched their pace in the street. Soon, inside the building, Albert Lloyd lit lamps and then opened the door to the back of the counter area.

'Get dollars in bags,' Fraser growled, 'and get to it fast.'

Albert Lloyd toiled for several minutes to stuff four sackcloth bags with close to ten thousand dollars. When he brought these up from the vaults, Fraser nodded.

'Now we leave,' he said, tension edging his words.

'Hell, Jake,' said Billy testily now. 'We've still got to get out of town. This man Sullivan – you reckon—'

'Keep her close,' spat Fraser, who'd accepted Hall's return to their partnership. 'She's our only means out.'

Billy nodded. 'We did it, Jake,' he said as he lifted one of the bags stuffed with money. 'We got our dreams.'

They exited the bank then, Billy with his gun levelled at TJ's head and Fraser jabbing his own Colt at Jeb, who maintained a guard in the road.

'Get three horses here fast, Sheriff,' he snapped. 'I want fresh mounts too.'

'Get to hell,' spat Jeb through gritted teeth. 'I already said you ain't leaving this town!'

'Goddamn it,' raged Fraser then, his eyes ablaze. 'I know you're right keen on this bitch, Sullivan.' He nodded at Billy, who stepped closer and jabbed his gun muzzle at TJ's eye. 'We'll kill her, Sullivan, don't make us do it.'

Jeb buckled then. He heard TJ's agonized, anguished cry and he cursed the ruse that Fraser and Hall had evidently used to draw them all in. Likely, these two outlaws had operated the same complex ways in other places,

ensuring murder and mayhem across the states and terri-
tories.

Cowing to Fraser's demands now, just wanting to keep
TJ alive, he moved along the street and got to the livery. In
time, with three mounts out of their stalls, he saddled
them. He gripped bunched reins in one hand and then
led the horses to the waiting outlaws.

Fraser grinned as he mounted, but kept his gun set on
Jeb. First, the now-mounted Billy rode, dragging the horse
TJ sat on with him. When they'd gotten to Driftwood's
edge, Billy whistled and Fraser laughed. He trotted his
horse to join them.

Jeb stood now seething with hate and despair. If he
launched forward, his gun drawn, seeking to end the lives
of Fraser and Hall, TJ would almost certainly lose her life.
He'd have to wait, pursue them across those night-swathed
plains.

'I love you, Jeb,' TJ's weak words drifted back out of the
dark beyond the town's edge now. 'I wanted us to marry!'

Fraser's mocking laugh came again then. 'Marry,' he
baited. 'Well, you sure can't marry in hell.'

Jeb lost control then. He turned and ran back towards
the livery, intent to mount a horse himself and rescue the
woman he loved. He halted after a few strides, though, as
an echoing roar sounded from the black grassland beyond
Driftwood's edge. Jeb turned, his head slumping, and he
battled the well of tears. He started to walk, retracing his
steps and heading out to find the body of the woman he
loved.

But he didn't make it to the end of the street. Suddenly,
two people walked side by side back into town, both
leading horses.

'I've brought back all the money and, I reckon, the woman you'll wed,' Billy proffered, throwing aside his gun. 'I treated her bad and I can't say sorry enough. I had to do it, though, to keep her alive!'

'You've switched sides before,' Jeb snapped, levelling his Colt. 'How do I—'

Billy jabbed a hand behind him. 'Fraser's horse is out there; all the money too.' He shoved a hand inside his shirt then and produced a small cloth bag. 'This is the three thousand dollars Fraser stole when he killed Scott. He also murdered a nice man name of Highwood at a farm some ways north.'

Soon, with Albert Lloyd garnering all the dollars and taking it to his bank, people began to drift back into Main Street. Many howled at the death and carnage that had beset the settlement. Whilst wives wept over the corpses of their loved ones, Jeb and TJ clutched each other tightly. When they finally parted, Jeb looked at the expectant faces of Mayor Collins and Sam Griffin.

'It's over,' he said with a nod. 'From this day forth Driftwood lives peaceful and free of trouble!'

'And Billy,' proffered Aaron with a smile. 'He did help me.'

Jeb shrugged. 'Hell, I ought to run you into a cell, Hall. I just don't—'

TJ cut in. 'He did save my life, Jeb, though he gave me a beating to do it!'

Billy looked pained. 'I've done wrong, Sullivan.' He jabbed a hand at the bodies littering the street. 'I never killed any. I got in with a psychopath I've just sent to hell. I want to make amends. I want my little farm and if you'll have me I'll settle here in Driftwood and do what I can to build this town again.'

Jeb, arm in arm with TJ then, walked along that street still curtained by gunsmoke.

Time passed as it always does. Decades later, when all the advances of the modern age had come to Driftwood and Billy Hall's ancestors populated the region as did those of Jeb and TJ, children would gather when the bell for school ended their day. They'd listen to the tales of that grey-whiskered old man who rocked in a chair outside the saloon.

Today, where Driftwood's Old West Graveyard is preserved as a monument to the town's founding fathers you'll find them all. That's all except for Fraser, of course. His corpse, dumped in an uncovered pit on the plains, ensured critters would devour him!

Aaron Auger survived, so the records attest, to be a hundred and one years old. Those Driftwood kids loved him; they loved his tales most of all – especially the one about the hellish Kansas storm.

Frail, his voice wavering, he'd nod at the kids gathered about him and rasp, 'It began that day a man called Jeb Sullivan dumped a corpse on the jail floor.' He'd wink then and drawl, 'After that, my little friends, it was a thunder of guns. . . .'